W9-BQS-337

Sown in Tears

Beverly Magid

Copyright © 2012 Beverly Magid
All rights reserved.

ISBN: I-478I-0457-0
ISBN-I3: 978I478I04575

Dedication

Dedicated to my two sets of grandparents

Who were brave enough to take the perilous journey to America,

Those who sow in tears will reap in glad joy. Psalm 126

ACKNOWLEDGEMENTS

I was lucky to have access to the YIVO archives in New York, with its books and photographs, as well as the enormous encyclopedia that they compiled in conjunction with Yale University. Additionally, two memoirs, *The Career of a Tsarist Officer* by Anton I. Denikin and *Days of Our Lives* by Rose Pesotta were extremely helpful. The trip I took to Russia and the Ukraine, arranged by Michael Masterovoy, at Master Travels, and his associate Nadia was essential, seeing the areas of former shtetls was so illuminating. The title of the book was inspired by a song, *Those Who Sow in Tears*, by the late, great Debbie Friedman.

Thanks to Marcia Newberger and Jennifer Hurley for their patient proofreading, the encouragement of writer friends to not stop writing when it all seemed impossible and the notes from Lynn Stegner, a wonderful writer and editor. This always leads me back to my initial mentor and cheerleader, Janet Fitch (White Oleander, Paint It Black), who said a long time ago that I should be writing novels. And so I have, even when I didn't know if they would ever see the light of day.

chapter I

THE SOUNDS GREW louder and closer. At first they were muffled as if wrapped in cotton wool, then they became sharper as guns cracked, horses whinnied, doors were smashed open, followed by the awful sounds of people screaming. But it was the heat that was the most alarming, waking Leah, as hot air surrounded her, invading the bedroom, making it difficult to breathe. The baby shrieked, and in his cot in the corner, eight-year-old Benny called out in terror, "Mama, mama."

Morris ran in as Leah jumped up from bed, where she had briefly slept fully dressed. Her husband was also dressed, his eyes red-rimmed, yelling, "Hurry Leah. They're here, they're burning houses."

He picked up Benny, who clutched his father's neck in a death-grip, his little body shaking, while Leah scooped up the baby, Joseph, his skin and thin cotton shirt drenched with sweat. Outside, fires cast an eerie red glow shining through the opening in the window covering, as they grabbed the bundles of clothes they had packed earlier that day. She looked around the room one last time, seeing the feather bed, Benny's cot, Joseph's cradle, wooden shelves holding their few clothes and Morris's prayer books, a pitcher of water next to the bed, alongside a pair of round metal-framed glasses.

Leah and Morris held their hands over the mouths of the children to keep them from crying out. They crept out of the house, then saw riders on horseback coming closer wielding knives, which gleamed silver in the cold, white moonlight. Down the steps into the cellar under the house, still cool, still safe for the moment. Before locking the door, Morris piled branches and twigs to camouflage the entrance.

It had been early that morning, that their neighbor Abraham Wolf had pounded on the door, warning that s roving band of peasants, an anti-Semitic band called the Black Hundreds, had attacked nearby villages, killing Jews and looting whatever they could. An attack on Koritz could at happen any time, so Morris remained on guard all day and then stayed awake all night, in case they came. Leah noted that for once, her husband didn't depend on just his faith in God to protect them. They stored fresh water and a basket with dried fruits, some vegetables, a loaf of bread and a jar of jam down in the cellar, along with the most precious of Morris's prayer books.

Now they huddled close on wooden crates in the cramped cellar space, the walls shaking as horses galloped by, the noise crashing over them like waves in a storm. It was too dangerous to light a candle, but Leah imagined their faces in the darkness, Morris choking on unaccustomed anger curdling like sour milk in his stomach, the baby stiff in her arms, exhausted from crying and little Benny, still clinging to Morris, his face buried in his father's neck.

Leah was bitter that they were paying the price of impossible conditions in Russia this year, 1905. The government had finally emancipated the serfs but the peasants had been pushed off the land they had farmed for generations, leaving many of them destitute. So they took their frustration and anger out on the Jews, since the authorities made sure to blame the Jews for all their troubles. Then in January, thousands of people gathered at the Winter Palace in St. Petersburg begging the Czar for better working conditions and an end to the disastrous war with Japan. But instead, the Czar left the city, leaving his troops to deal with the protests. Unnerved by the numbers of people, they fired on the unarmed protesters killing hundreds.

Here in the Settlement of the Pale, the area where the government forced most Jews to live, life was hard, but in times of real trouble, Leah thought, it was always worse for the Jews. No matter what the real truth, the Jews were used as scapegoats by the authorities, who encouraged the state newspapers to print government lies which the people believed. Outrageous lies like the blood libel, accusing Jews of using the blood of Christian children in the making of their Passover matzos or accusing Jews of working with the Japanese to defeat Russia in the war.

This day had started as an ordinary day, but a happy one, Benny's eighth birthday. She had saved an egg and baked a small cake for his special birthday breakfast. He tried to slip back under the covers in order to avoid his daily chores of drawing water from the well and feeding the chickens. It was hard not to laugh at his antics. With his large dark eyes fringed by long lashes, he resembled her brother Dov, except for the ears, which stuck out like the handles on a milk jug.

Today was also going to be Morris's first day of working at Holstein's mill, keeping the accounts. His first steady job, which he finally agreed to take, even if it infringed on his routine of study and prayers. When she agreed to marry him ten long years ago, Fanny, the marriage broker, neglected to mention his fanatic devotion to Torah study over wages. Families with money could afford to keep a son-in-law at home to study, but although both she and her father valued learning, her father could not afford to keep them. Morris had no family of his own, so they had been struggling financially all through their marriage.

They couldn't leave the cellar until they were sure that the attackers were gone. Looters would be ransacking houses looking for anything of value. Leah buried their only treasures, a silver Kiddush cup and spice box, wedding presents from her family, underneath the chicken coops in the shed. Her strategy was to leave an item for the looters to find. "If they've scavenged something," she said to Morris, "maybe they'll be satisfied and go without destroying everything." She thought about leaving her silver and tortoise-shell combs, but this was a gift handed down from mother to daughter for generations. Once she hoped to give it to her own daughter, but baby Rachel didn't survive her first month and now lay buried in the cemetery outside town. The death of Rachel and two other still-born baby girls, remained a wound that wouldn't heal, that time continued to pick at, like scabs that continued to pull at the skin, even though she went on to give birth to Benny and Joseph. The combs were safe in her apron pocket, and instead she left the brass samovar, the tea pot still sitting on top, filled with strong tea, hoping that would placate the attackers.

Another horse rumbled over-head, shaking powdery dust from the cellar walls and Leah leaned over to protect Joseph's face and body. Their household was a meager one and she jumped at each sound of dishes breaking, praying that the oven might be spared. She thought of all the family dinners she had cooked there, even the Sabbaths when Morris might invite a homeless person for *Shabbos* dinner, ignoring the fact that there was little more than a taste of meat for his own family.

"Leah," he would say as he ushered in some gaunt-looking old man in tattered clothes, ignoring the grim expression on her face, "set another place. We're honored to have a guest for Shabbos."

She removed Joseph's soiled diaper, wet the bottom of her skirt with water to sponge and soothe his skin. Wrapping a clean cloth around him, she unbuttoned her dress and let him nurse, feeling his body relax, hearing his breathing become steady until he fell asleep.

Morris continued praying and, to Leah, each word he sent to God was a betrayal of her. God did not protect Koritz from this pogrom. These murderers attacked because they could, because Czar Nicholas didn't care two kopeks about a rampage that killed only Jews. Soldiers and unhappy peasants alike were encouraged to consider Jews as righteous targets for slaughter. Cycles of violence against the Jews were a legacy of Russian history. It had taken just one false accusation circulated in the papers that Jews had collaborated with the enemy to start it all over again.

"Enough, Morris," she snapped, shifting the baby to her other arm. "You saved us, not your indifferent God."

"Hush, Leah. It's not for us to question Him."

She saw him reach in his pocket for his reading glasses, but then realized that he had left them next to the bed. It didn't matter, he could recite most of the prayers from memory. He was a gentle man; she appreciated that quality, but it infuriated her that he could depend so completely on a deity that totally ignored him.

Morris opened a slat which covered a tiny crack in the wall hoping for a little fresh air. A sliver of moonlight streamed in, shedding a little light in the darkness. Voices continued to shout as shots rang out. The smell of smoke grew stronger and Morris quickly replaced the slat.

Despite the noise, the damp mustiness of the cellar lulled the children into a restless dozing. Even Morris began to nod. But Leah had no such easy escape. How did she get to this place, this time of horror? What would happen to them? Would her father and brothers ever know, grieve for their little

Leah? Alarmed by each new sound, she was afraid of what they would find when they emerged from this hole in the ground. She recognized the voice of a neighbor, Mrs. Rodinsky, cursing someone on horseback, as they rode roughshod through her vegetable garden.

A scream ripped apart the night, waking Morris and the children, the baby wailing before either Leah or Morris could clap a hand over his mouth. She held her breath, when suddenly there was a pounding on the cellar door. No one moved, but the door broke open and Leah saw the outline of a man in a long military coat, holding a sword reflecting the glow of the fires outside. The intruder pushed into their hiding place, crowding the small space. Before Leah could move even her smallest finger, before she had time to exhale a wisp of breath, Morris pushed Benny behind him, as the sword plunged into his chest, his thin body crumpling forward without a sound. Benny fell with Morris, still clinging to his father's leg, his large eyes wide with terror at seeing blood stream from Morris's wound.

Leah's breath choked in her chest, bile gagging in her throat, but she made herself breathe when she saw the soldier raise his arm, ready to strike again.

"Wait, please," she cried, forcing the words out of her mouth. "Wait. See what I have for you."

She reached into her apron pocket, taking out the silver and tortoise-shell combs, stretching her hand towards him, seeing his eyes light up at the prospect of further spoils. "Let us go, please," she said, her fingers tightly clasping the combs, watching every movement in the man's face, every shadow passing over his eyes. Behind him the moon shone through the open door. He was young, no more than twenty, sparse, drooping moustaches making him look even younger, cheeks splattered with blood, while his eyes fixated on the combs. He was probably the same age as her brother Dov the last time she saw him back in Yanov, when she left to marry Morris.

"Think how beautiful they would be on your sweetheart," she said, "or even your mother. Take them, but let us go, please." How she wanted to rip off those moustaches and cause him great pain, but instead she spoke quietly, soothingly, as if she were a mother comforting a restless child.

Another soldier peered into the cellar. "Kill them and let's get out of here." But the younger one seemed mesmerized by Leah, as she held Joseph tightly with one hand and slowly released her grip on the combs with the other. They stared at each other for a very long minute, while Leah silently prayed to that God who never listened.

"No," the young soldier finally said. "I don't have to kill them. They'll probably starve to death anyway." He took the combs, wheeled about abruptly and left.

Leah laid the baby down on the quilt and rushed to Morris, looking for any signs of life. He barely breathed, blood oozed from his chest, spittle stained his beard. It was urgent to find Anna Vashenko, the mid-wife, who might be able to help. But how could she leave the children alone in the midst of all this horror? She took a clean cloth and pressed on the wound, but couldn't staunch the bleeding. She had to find Anna now or Morris would die.

"Benny, put your hands here and press hard. I'm going to get help for Papa." Benny slowly sat up, afraid to look at his father. "Benny, do what I tell you," she repeated sternly. The boy took a deep breath and pressed on the cloth with both his hands.

Leah crept to the cellar door and peered out, ready to slam it shut if she saw anyone moving about. Their house had been attacked, the front door hacked open, the windows smashed. A little ways beyond, she saw Mrs. Rodinsky sitting in the midst of her uprooted garden, the moon shining on her tear-streaked face, arms wrapped around her chest, soaked in blood. But Leah couldn't stop, not now, not if there was a chance that Morris could be helped. She had to find Anna. She ran through the narrow cobblestone alleys between the houses, down the main road, onto a side path, hearing the sounds of riders and horses recede into the night. She kept low and out of sight, making her way past houses which had been wrecked as if a giant hand had played a game with them, making them fall.

The door of Anna's house stood open like a gaping wound, the shed next to it, empty of the cow and all the chickens. "Anna, Anna Vashenko, it's me, Leah Peretz. Please, Anna, don't be afraid, I need your help." There was no answer. Someone on horseback galloped past and Leah ran to the shed, tripping over a body, lying next to a leather satchel, its contents scattered. It was Anna, a long bloody gash across her neck, her body lifeless on the ground. There was no sign of life. This gentle woman, who had attended Leah at all her births, Rachel, Benny, Joseph, as well as the two stillborn girls. In lieu of a doctor, Anna prescribed herbs for all the ills of the village.

"Oh, my dear Anna, what will we do without you?" Leah whispered.

Leah had not seen any neighbors except for Mrs. Rodinsky. Now there were no more sounds of gunfire, or screams piercing the night, it was strangely quiet. Not even a hoot from an errant barn owl. The world was silent as death. Where was everybody? Were they all dead? Leah collapsed next to Anna, her face wet with tears. She made herself stand, she had to get back to the children and Morris.

She scooped up all the medicines, herbs, vials, stuffing everything back into Anna's bag. On the way home a face peered out from behind the rubble, but quickly hid again as she passed by. The air was acrid with the smell of smoke. Many houses were made of wood, with thatched roofs, it took only a spark to turn them into bonfires. As she neared her house Leah saw that Mrs. Rodinsky had slid onto her side, eyes open, staring lifeless at her torn-up garden. Leah held her breath and gently closed the woman's eyes.

A voice in the darkness called out weakly, "Leah, is that you?" Sophia Wolf limped towards her, like a frightened lost child, her hair uncovered, exposing her shaved head. Leah had never seen her without a wig or head covering. She was like a ghostly scarecrow moving towards her.

"Sophia, are you hurt?" Leah asked, alarmed by her neighbor's appearance. "Where is Abraham?"

The woman fell to her knees. "Abraham made me hide in the hayloft, while he went looking for Isaac. The soldiers killed them both."

"Oh God, it was a soldier that killed Morris," Leah said. Did the same boy continue his killing spree after sparing her and the children? "Come with me, Sophia. I have to see to Morris. He's badly hurt."

Leah went down the cellar steps, softly calling, "Benny, sweetheart, it's Mama." She found him in the corner, cowering against a large bag of potatoes, but still pressing the cloth against his father's chest.

Morris's eyes fluttered but did not open, his face the color of freshly ground flour. "Morris," she whispered into his ear. "Morris, it's Leah." She pressed her own hand on the wound, feeling the blood thick and warm on her fingers. Morris did not respond.

Taking her hand away for an instant, she emptied the bag of medicines, desperate to know which salve or powder Anna would have used. The baby whimpered, shivering on the quilt, reeking of urine. She directed Benny to get one of Morris's shirts, and while Benny pressed against Morris's wound, she sponged and changed the baby. Then she tore off a small strip of clean cloth and dipped it into the jar of jam and gave it to the baby to suck on. Turning back to Morris, she untied the scarf covering her hair, sprinkled a dark powder on it and applied it to the wound.

Unlike Sophia, Leah's own hair was unshorn, still thick and auburn, because she had refused to shave it when she married, rebelling against the Orthodox tradition. Morris had ranted and argued but she swore that she would keep her head covered at all times with a scarf. Her hair was just one of the many arguments that she and Morris had right from the beginning. First it was her hair, then her books, novels that he tried to ban. And of course they always quarreled about money, his refusing to take a steady job, instead relying on sporadic teaching assignments. He liked to remind her that she had consented to marry a Torah scholar. All those sharp words seemed unimportant now as he lay mortally wounded at her feet.

"Benny, go tell Sophia to come down and rest here." But the boy hid behind her, shaking his head. "Do as I say," she said sharply. "We have no time for arguments."

Snuffling, the boy crawled up the steps. Leah heard him whisper, "Mrs. Wolf, Mama says to come in and rest." But Sophia refused to move.

Leah applied new poultices to Morris's wound during the night, keeping him warm, listening for any changes in his breathing. She held his hand, trying to be reassuring, but the words didn't come easily, just the pressure of her fingers. Suddenly there was a loud gurgling in his throat, then, silence. She put her ear next to his mouth, hoping to hear or feel a whisper of breath on her skin. His pasty-white color turned bluish as if he were being pressed under ice.

"Morris." She whispered his name again and again, hoping to entice him back from that dark, icy place he had entered.

Benny sobbed, his fists jammed against his eyes. Leah and the boy clung tightly together for a long time, until she told Benny to kiss Morris goodbye.

"No, no Mama." The boy shrank back against her.

"Come, let's do it together," she said. "Papa saved our lives; we must show him our love." She took Benny's hand and gently pulled him towards Morris. First she leaned over and pressed her lips to his forehead, then told Benny to do the same. She watched as the boy bent down to kiss his father, then pulled him back onto her lap, gently caressing the boy's cheek.

There would be no time for any real mourning. Jewish law insisted that the dead be interred as quickly as possible, and now for reasons of health it was even more imperative. In the aftermath, there would be no one available to do burial rituals, so it was up to Leah to clean away the blood, remove his jacket and wrap Morris in his *talis*, knowing he would want to be buried in his prayer shawl. If Sophia helped, they could also bury Abraham and Isaac. Tonight, she and Benny would keep watch over Morris's body and honor him by reciting psalms until it got light. She turned to Psalm 126, reading, "Those who tearfully sow will reap in glad song," but the promise of relief was nothing more than a meaningless jumble of symbols on the page.

As dawn lighted the new day, she left to scout a cart and shovel, but Benny refused to stay alone with the body. She held him, quietly comforting him. "We must bury Papa, Benny. I need you to be brave and help me."

He followed close at her side and they went outside together, with Joseph slung in a shawl, tied across her shoulder. At the cellar entrance, they found Sophia in the same place, arms still wrapped around her knees.

"Sophia, come with me. We're going to bury Morris and then we'll also bury Abraham and Isaac."

Leah worried about what Benny would see in the aftermath of the attack, the bodies of the dead still laying in the mud, where they had fallen, one looking as if he had tumbled out of his house, slipping on an icy step, stretched out at his front door.

She insisted that Benny keep his eyes straight ahead, avoiding looking either right or left, as they went to the cemetery. In one night his childhood was over. All her dreams of giving him an easier childhood than she had had, modest but filled with books and learning and love had vanished with the flash of a soldier's sword.

Sophia looked baffled, but did as she was told, following Leah to the remains of the shed. A shovel hung next to the empty chicken coops and the cart was miraculously still intact. In the Wolfs' barn, Leah found a second shovel and noticed that even though Sophia's house had been destroyed, her small barn could be used as shelter

Filled with great dread, Leah entered the remains of her own home. The door was gone, the windows smashed, the oven battered and useless, the table and chairs reduced to kindling. Only a few cups were left unbroken. Feathers from the ripped bed and quilt drifted in the air like snowflakes while Benny's cot and the cradle, so lovingly carved by Morris for their first-born Rachel, lay in pieces. She stepped over slivers of glass and saw the twisted metal that was all that remained of Morris's glasses.

Ten years of her life had been spent in the small confines of this house. It had all started with Fanny the Matchmaker who only told Leah and her father that the groom was eleven years older and very learned. Fanny told Morris even less, not wanting to scare him away by mentioning how rebellious his bride was even at sixteen. Leah traveled to Koritz excited by the chance for a new life. Morris met her carriage and took her directly to the Rabbi's house to have the ceremony performed. Almost immediately they had had their first argument over the cutting of her hair.

"I won't wear those ugly wigs and I won't shave my head," she had shouted. Morris spoke quietly at first, then with greater force. "It's an outrage." That was the prelude to their first night together. Perhaps their marriage had never recovered from that first dispute. An uneasy truce made their days possible and their nights stonily tolerable.

Leah and Benny, with very little aid from Sophia, used the cart to transport the bodies of Morris, Abraham and the Wolfs' son Isaac, requiring three trips to complete their sad duty. She was horrified to see that at the cemetery some of the headstones had been overturned by the attackers and quickly checked the little corner of the graveyard where baby Rachel was buried. Thankfully her grave had been spared.

The ground was winter hard, the wind moaned as if the earth was crying over the deaths. It wasn't easy to dig the graves. Benny wasn't strong enough and Sophia sat herself on the ground counting out imaginary utensils, as if she were at home making an inventory of dinnerware. When it was time to lower Morris into the ground, Leah regretted that she had not said something more loving to him before he died. Benny recited Kaddish as she shoveled in the dirt and she whispered "Goodbye and God bless," wondering if the dead might not be more blessed now than the living.

Back at the cellar after their long, difficult day, she sat watching Joseph, sleeping peacefully, snuggling in Morris's shirt covered by a wool shawl she had rescued from the house. Benny, exhausted by his death duties, tossed and turned, stranded somewhere between tearful sleep and roiling nightmares. He would cry out "Papa," and then would be still.

Sophia refused to enter the cellar and stayed alone in her barn, propped against the stall where her cow once lived. She was too terrified to even lie down, panicked that the mobs might return to continue the killing they had begun the previous night.

Leah fed the children and tried unsuccessfully to get Sophia to eat. Now she collapsed in a heap next to her boys. Although she was desperate for sleep, worries about getting more food kept her awake. There was little space for any real comfort in the cellar, but the barn was too cold for the children, so she and the boys huddled close together, conserving the little bit of warmth they could muster.

chapter 2

CAPTAIN IVAN VASELIK wasn't enjoying his morning tea, no matter how many lumps of sugar he added to the glass. This was going to be a hellish day and he wasn't looking forward to it. He liked order in his life, in his command, with the soldiers under his control. The possibility of a pogrom made everything messy, no matter what Moscow might think. He had received reports that there had been attacks on two nearby villages by roving bands, probably the one called the Black Hundreds.

He was no lover of Jews, but his men could be tempted to join with the peasants in the violence and lootings, like other soldiers and Cossacks had done before. Vaselik might not care one way or the other about their participation, but he didn't like having to clean up the aftermath that these attacks invariably brought. Soldiers out of control could turn mutinous, which had occurred in other garrisons and had to be avoided at all costs. Today's soldier was an unstable thing, one that needed to be tightly reined in.

Instead of the posting at Koritz, Vaselik had always expected a more prestigious assignment in Moscow or St. Petersburg, where an officer's talents were recognized and he could reap suitable rewards and attention. If he had attended the Royal Military Academy, he would never have been posted to this no-account camp. Even a combat assignment would have been better. War provided opportunity for advancement.

Instead he looked around his office, which was as cramped and as shabby as any of the shacks the poorest Jews in town occupied. It was stripped down to the bare essentials, a desk, with his predecessor's initials carved on the side, two hard-backed chairs and a wooden cabinet, where he kept files and an extra supply of vodka. Without a good drink, he sometimes wondered if he'd be able to survive this god forsaken place.

But instead of dwelling on lost opportunities, this morning he needed to concentrate on protecting his present situation from any possible dangers.

"Sasha," he roared. "I want everyone in dress parade in ten minutes." There was no reply. "Did you hear me?"

"Yes Captain," Sasha answered from the other room. "It will be done." The orderly sighed, a sound which should have been inaudible but of course Vaselik heard it and came charging to the doorway.

"Is there a problem?" he asked, towering over his nervous orderly. Vaselik's black eyes narrowed their focus on Sasha's round face, which looked as if it might implode in fear.

"N-n-no sir. Everything is fine."

As Sasha scurried off, Vaselik yelled, "Make sure my own horse is ready for me."

Was he the only captain in the Russian army with a timid mouse for an orderly, while up and down the countryside his peers were aided by hungry wolves, who bargained on their behalf for cases of vodka, sides of beef, barrels of potatoes and introductions to the prettiest of the neighborhood ladies? And the junior officers under his command were no better. Sometimes he was sure that life conspired against him.

Life was beginning to spin out of control, he thought. Peasants rising up, soldiers shooting unarmed citizens, Russia losing a war to the Japanese. It was as if he had awakened to find out that his worst nightmare was a reality.

After everyone lined up, Vaselik mounted his stallion, Nicodemus, raking his glance over the men and horses. Properly led, these men should be able to handle any trouble that a roving band of peasants might cause, especially if he allowed them to "liberate" some of the Jewish spoils. But he would not tolerate any violence from his men, no matter how he felt about Jews. It was mandatory that things stay somewhat under control.

The troops rode in single file through the village, Vaselik in the lead, demonstrating to everyone that all was well and peaceful, until Abraham

Wolf came running up, causing Nicodemus to nervously rear. The man stood, cap in hand, a respectful look on his face.

"Captain, sir, I hope we can count on your help should anything happen tonight." The man acted submissive, but Vaselik saw a small vein in Wolf's forehead pulsate, showing that anger roiled just below the surface.

"Wolf, as you can see, my men are well prepared."

"Yes, sir, but I have heard that in other towns, soldiers sometimes joined the peasants." Abraham stepped back as Nicodemus reared up again.

"Careful, man. Can't you see you're upsetting the horse?" If he were in Moscow right now, Vaselik thought, he might have been assigned to the Royal Guards. "The only problem," he said, "that could occur is if some rogue Cossack comes into town with these other bandits. The Cossacks are hard to control."

"Then Captain, we Jews will have to take steps to protect ourselves." Abraham stepped back to let the column pass by.

"Lawbreakers will be punished, no matter who they are," Vaselik shouted over his shoulder as he continued his tour.

chapter 3

Leah walked through the village. With Joseph nestled against her chest, wrapped in a shawl. Benny held her hand, shivering despite a jacket and a thick sweater. The morning sun shone brightly, but it was a wintry sun, giving no warmth, good only for illuminating the scene of destruction. She had always regarded Koritz as a tiny pinprick at the end of the world, possessing none of the charm of her childhood village, Yanov, with its apple orchards, meadows bordering the Pripyet River. Now after the attack, Koritz literally resembled the end of the world. A few houses constructed of brick still stood mostly intact, but many wooden structures, like hers, had caught fire and been destroyed. A stench of death hovered over the village, corpses still unburied, perhaps lost under the debris, bodies of animals caught in the cross-fire. If the Jews were called The Chosen People, was this what they had been chosen for?

She searched for familiar faces: Solomon Weiss, the baker, her neighbor, Gittel, Androvsky the *shochet*, the kosher slaughterer, the Rebbe, or his *shamus*, Samuel. It was the gentle Samuel who walked through Koritz every Friday, announcing the coming of the Sabbath, alerting everyone to the exact time to suspend all work. Then, at last, she spotted Solomon's wife, Yetta, picking through the ashes of her house, tears streaming down her face, clutching a scorched pot, as if it was a family treasure.

The two women embraced and Leah hesitated, "Are you and Solomon both safe?"

Yetta slowly shook her head no. "My fool of a husband tried to protect the ovens and those pigs shot him. All he had was a stick to fight them off. But thank God he's alive." She wiped her eyes and asked, "What about Morris?"

"A soldier broke into the cellar where we were hiding," Leah said, unable to finish, letting her face tell the rest of the story.

"Papa died saving our lives," Benny whispered. He hid his face in the folds of Leah's skirt, trying to be brave and not let the women see him cry.

Hearing Benny say out loud the words, "Papa died," made it painfully real. It wasn't just the awful dreams she had at night or a newspaper account of war and death. It had really happened to her and the children. Morris was dead and she was left head of the family.

"Abraham Wolf was killed," Leah said, "and Mrs. Rodinsky and Anna Vashenko." Yetta gasped at the enormity of it all and the two women clung to each other and wept.

Benny tugged at his mother's dress, motioning for her to lean down. He said softly, "Mama, I'm hungry." His breakfast had consisted only of a little dried fruit and a small piece of bread. That had been hours earlier.

"Yetta," Leah pleaded, "have you seen anyone with food? We saved only a little down in the cellar. But I have a bushel of potatoes I could trade for milk or eggs or maybe a little meat."

"Try to find Leon, he still has one of his cows," Yetta said. "Maybe he could give you some milk. I'm sorry, I have nothing to offer. They not only broke the ovens, they stole all the bread."

Leah remembered Solomon's golden challahs, filled with plump raisins and his holiday cakes dusted with sugar, fruit nestled inside. He was famous in Koritz and beyond. Sometimes when she had a few extra kopeks, she treated the family to one of his sugar crusted cakes. He pretended it didn't matter, but his wide smile showed how proud he was seeing the number of women who lined up for his baked works of art.

An old man hobbled very slowly towards them. It was the Rebbe, a man known for his immaculate long, black coat and fur *streimel*. Today, his clothes were disheveled, covered in dust, no hat or *kippah*, thin strands of hair barely criss-crossing his head, while he kept his hands clasped in front of him, as if in perpetual prayer.

"Have either of you seen my shamus, Samuel?" His eyes glistened red and rheumy, his step shuffling and unsteady. He plucked at his beard, leaving empty raw patches where he pulled hairs from his cheeks.

"Where's the *Rebetzen*, Rabbi?" Leah asked. If his wife were well, she would never let him wander about in this condition. Please, Leah thought, I cannot bear to hear another tale of death or injury. No family in Koritz was untouched by the calamity. Where were the authorities, what happened to the village's so-called friend, Captain Vaselik, commander of the Cavalry Brigade? Jews were forced to live in these areas and they were vulnerable without military support.

"The *Rebetzen*?" The old man seemed confused by the question, as if Leah had asked after Czarina Alexandra. His face scrunched like a baby about to cry, but instead he walked off muttering that he had to find Samuel.

Benny pulled again at Leah's skirt. "I know, Benny, I'm doing the best I can."

Her body suddenly buckled, sagging down abruptly onto a large rock at the side of the road. How could she possibly manage? If only they had run away instead of hiding, if Morris hadn't relied on God to save them. She could barely breathe. Leah turned to speak to Yetta, but the woman was back at the shell that once was her home, searching to find just one more possession.

✳✳✳

Four young recruits stood at attention in front of Captain Vaselik. He sat astride his horse, the animal's flanks steamy with sweat even in the cold morning air. The four had been standing at attention for over an hour waiting for Vaselik to return from his morning gallop and an inspection of the town's devastation. He did not look happy with the men or with what he had just seen.

Vaselik had inferred from the information sent by Moscow that the military should try to rein in any peasant uprising against the Jewish population, but the authorities really did not care if they were successful. His soldiers knew that if they happened to "come upon" goods from Jewish households, they could "liberate" them with impunity, as long as they were not directly involved with violence. But he had heard rumors that two of them might have been responsible for the deaths of Morris Peretz, Abraham Wolf and his son Isaac. Nothing had been proven, but still his patience was stretched beyond its limits.

"It has come to my attention that you disobeyed my explicit orders not to get involved in any violence, directly or indirectly. Your punishment will be forfeiting half your pay for three months and doing extra duty, including helping to keep the place clean, especially the latrines.

In addition, I want to see all of the spoils you took. And don't hold anything back."

A pile of farm tools, four chickens, twenty-five kopeks, a gold wedding band and a pair of woman's combs soon appeared on Vaselik's desk. Not much to show for the death of three people, even Jews. But he would see that some of this was returned to the two widows. He felt somewhat cheered by the time Sasha brought in his midday meal of a steaming bowl of borscht and a loaf of dark bread.

Still, Vaselik needed to ride again this afternoon. His morning ride had not completely calmed his mood. Usually, by six o'clock he finished breakfast and rode Nicademus hard for an hour before returning to the barracks. But since the attack three days ago, his regular routines had been upset, disturbing both horse and rider. Now as he mounted him, he could feel the animal's frustration at being held back, so he gave him his head to gallop across the fields towards the forest several miles away.

On the way back, he spied the slight figure of a woman moving slowly on the main road. As he came closer he saw she was carrying a baby wrapped in a wool shawl, while a young boy held fast to her hand. At the sound of the hoofs pounding towards them, they froze in place, a look of terror flashed across both their faces

"I'm sorry if I frightened you," he said. recognizing Leah, the widow of Morris Peretz. "How are you, Mrs. Peretz?"

"How should I be, Captain," Leah snapped, "considering my husband was killed by one of your men." Although she kept her voice even, there was no mistaking her rage.

"You're quite mistaken," Vaselik said. "It could not have been one of my soldiers. They were under strict orders. Perhaps you mistook one of the

Cossacks who sometimes ride with the peasants. However, I wish to help you, even though I know nothing can make up for your loss." His face reddened at how easily he lied, angry that this woman made him feel any guilt.

"I saw him with my own eyes," she said.

Nicodemus pawed at the ground, nervous at being reined in, and Vaselik was also anxious to get away from those accusing eyes.

"I tell you it must have been a Cossack. Come to the post," he said brusquely, his breath etched in the cold air. "I'll see that you receive some money and chickens. And tell Abraham Wolf's wife to come as well."

Leah's face registered surprise, but before she could reply, Vaselik touched the sides of the horse with his heels and galloped off across the field.

chapter 4

PEOPLE WERE GATHERING in the town square. Everyone looked for relatives, friends, neighbors, anyone who could reassure them that life might become normal again. Leah surveyed the scene, crowded and chaotic, right out of one of her novels, "War and Peace."

Hannah Gold screamed in joy when she found that her sister had managed to escape during that fateful night, while Solomon Schneider stood by wordlessly, unable to comprehend that his son and daughter-in-law had died when their house was torched. Leah could not bear to watch any more. The town's small cemetery outside town would soon be bulging with the corpses of villagers who just three days ago ate, worked, gossiped, sometimes flirted, occasionally even danced in life. Every night she was being haunted by the specter of Morris's blood-spattered face and awoke feeling guilty for not having saved him.

The nervousness of the people was evident as they constantly looked over their shoulders, ready to flee at an unexpected noise, or a face they didn't immediately trust. Unable to leave them at home, Leah carried Joseph, with Benny by her side. The children had become physical appendages, attached to her body, reminding her of those months when they grew in her womb, sustained only by her blood and breath. Benny refused to leave her and the baby fussed and whimpered, so unlike his placid nature. Their demands gave Leah no respite, as if the night of the attack had never ended.

Before the assault, the square had been bounded on one side by the synagogue, a simple wood building, but the proud possessor of an ancient Torah, protected in heavy red velvet, topped with an ornate silver crown.

Next door was Haim Holstein's house, a two storey, red brick building, having the place of honor next to the shul, as befitted the owner of the mill and acknowledged leader of Koritz. Although the Holstein house still stood, there were gaping holes instead of windows and through the broken glass she could see that the downstairs salon was charred and smoky, while the synagogue had been turned into a pile of charred ash. On the other side of the synagogue had been the *mikvah*, the place for ritual bathing, where Leah floated in peace and serenity each month after her menses, a required time for purification, which she had cherished for its solitude. Many of the strictures of Orthodox traditions chafed at her, but the mikvah was her personal sanctuary, a place where she could remember a time of innocence. Now that too was gone.

This is where, once a week, the square was turned into the market place, where women bargained and traded. Like them, Leah sold eggs and home-grown vegetables to supplement the small amount Morris earned tutoring Hebrew. Sometimes she managed to wheedle an extra piece of meat or an additional bag of fruit. Poverty had made her a shrewd bargainer.

Holstein moved through the crowd, greeting people, patting the heads of small children, almost as if he were running for office. Over six feet tall, he easily jumped up atop a cart, held steady by two other men, and called out to the assembled crowd.

"Neighbors of Koritz," he said, "this is a terrible time for us all. Many of our loved ones are injured or dead. Those of us who are left must help each other."

People nodded their heads in agreement, but Leah wondered what people had left to give.

Holstein continued, "They may have wrecked my mill, but they didn't carry away all the grain or flour, so I will divide what's left into a small portion for every family, and in return, I ask for your help to repair the damage. Now who else has supplies to share?"

Leon Lipski spoke up, "As long as my cow gives milk, anybody can come get a cup." Devorah Mayer called out, "I have some extra children's things, maybe a little worn." Leah and others laughed, knowing that since Devorah's ten children ranged from twelve years to six months, the clothes she offered would be more than just a little worn. Still, Leah hoped to trade potatoes for a sweater for Joseph and a pair of shoes for Benny. Holstein exhorted the crowd to remember that the Torah mandated Jews to help each other. "He who gives some of his food to the poor, he shall be blessed."

Since she had Anna Vashenko's medicines, Leah called out asking if anyone knew what each herb was used for. No one spoke up, until her neighbor, Gittel, remembered that Anna had been taught by old woman, Freydel, a healer who lived on the outskirts of the forest.

"If Freydel is still alive," Gittel said, "she could probably tell you."

A line of people, hoping to get a portion of flour, began snaking around the square and when it was Leah's turn, Holstein himself came over to measure out her portion.

"I was so sorry to hear about Morris," he said, "If there is anything I can do to help, please let me know."

She was grateful for his attention. "Perhaps when the mill starts again, you could hire me for Morris's job."

"You're good with numbers?" His surprise acknowledged that he wasn't convinced that a woman would be able to add and subtract.

"Yes, of course," she said sharply. "And I also speak and write Russian." Perhaps it was a touch of vanity but she had to remind him that she came from an educated family. Of course, not everyone in the village thought that knowing Russian was an asset and some of the ultra religious had complained about her to Morris.

"It's a disgrace to speak that language. Yiddish is good enough for us," one member of the synagogue had complained. In his calm, stoic way, Morris simply deflected their anger, surprising Leah by his defense of her.

"Am I supposed to rebuke her for having knowledge?" he said. "God appreciates a learned mind."

After getting the flour, she searched for Leon and traded for milk, then found Devorah to barter for the coveted sweater and shoes, promising them both to return with some potatoes. Back home, she checked on Sophia, who still lay curled in a fetal position in the barn. Since they buried her husband and son, she had not moved from her pallet. She refused to eat, keeping her lips tightly closed, except occasionally to sip some water.

It was hard to believe that this Sophia was the same lively woman who had taken so much pride in her sewing, in the Talmudic accomplishments of her son Isaac. Isaac was about to be matched with a girl from a neighboring village, considered a prize catch. Now Sophia was disappearing a little bit each day.

Holstein had recruited teams of men to clear debris and help patch houses which could be made habitable again and others to search for bodies. Leah constantly worried about the dead that still hadn't been properly buried. Without a doctor or Anna Vashenko, Koritz would be helpless against the spread of any disease throughout the shtetl. If it were possible, Leah would have kept Joseph and Benny isolated from the outside world, but she wouldn't risk leaving them alone even when she searched for food. In better times, she could have trusted eight-year-old Benny to watch the baby for short periods, but now he was too terrified to stop clinging to her. Noises panicked him, the sight of strangers made him ill.

So although it was a trek of several miles to Freydel's house, Leah determined to see her as soon as possible. She dressed Joseph in his new sweater, wrapping him securely in a shawl which she slung across her shoulder. Benny now had shoes without torn soles and she used strips of clean cloth to cover his feet, since there were no stockings to go with the shoes. Then, with Anna's satchel under her arm, she and the children set off to see Freydel.

As they trudged through town, they passed patches of snow heaped on each side of the road, blackened by soot and ash from the fires. Once outside the village, the air became fresh and untainted, the world was swaddled in whiteness, like a newborn baby. Off in the distance, tall spruce trees dazzled, their branches dripping sparkling crystals.

"Let's stop a minute, Benny. Look how beautiful it all looks. No smells of smoke, no ugly burnt out houses. God is giving us a second chance."

Leah might dispute God herself, having wrestled with Him all her life, like Jacob battling the angel, never forgiving Him for her mother's slow debilitating illness or now the horror of the pogrom, but she knew how strong the bond that Morris had forged between Benny and God. To deny that would break the boy's heart, like renouncing Morris himself. Morris's relationship with Benny was so close that she was often envious of them. She'd see them studying together, heads touching, feeling a little shut out.

Freydel's house crouched behind a row of birch trees, tall white-barked sentinels, the door peeking out between them. Leah knocked softly at first, then harder, but no one answered. No smoke rose from the chimney, nor was there any other sign that someone was at home, except that a pathway had recently been cleared of snow and dry pine needles strewn along the walk.

"Freydel, it is Leah Peretz, from Koritz. Please open the door." Leah stamped her feet to keep warm, drawing Benny and Joseph closer to shield them from the day's damp chill.

Cautiously, the door opened a crack and a voice whispered, "Are you alone?"

"Yes, Freydel. Except for my two children, I'm alone. But it's very cold out here. Please let us in."

The crack widened and the old woman motioned them inside and quickly shut the door. The scarf tied around her head did not totally hide tufts of iron grey hair. Her eyes, bright blue and as penetrating as two bullets shot from a gun, were set in a heavily lined face. The villagers in Koritz estimated Freydel the Healer to be over eighty, but those fiery eyes showed no signs of passing time. For years she had lived alone, healing all who came to her door. Nobody remembered if she had ever had a husband or children. She never talked about her past.

"Is the trouble in Koritz over?" she asked.

"The killing and burning have stopped if that's what you mean," Leah said. "But I'm afraid that the real trouble starts now with little food and many dead still unburied."

"I heard them passing my house, yelling and shooting off their guns. Why they didn't stop I don't know. But I didn't even light a fire to boil water," Freydel said. "I was afraid someone would see the smoke and decide to cut my throat thinking I had gold hidden somewhere in the house. This isn't the first trouble I've lived through. And it probably won't be the last."

She lit the samovar and began brewing tea, also cutting thick slices of bread, slathering on cherry preserves. She handed a slice each to Leah and Benny and gave Joseph a small piece to chew on. Leah ate slowly, but Benny swallowed his in a few bites, looking up hopefully at Freydel. Her face unfolded into a smiling accordion of wrinkles, as she cut him another piece.

"No Benny, we mustn't be greedy" Leah said, giving the bread back to Freydel. "One slice is enough."

"Let the boy eat, Leah. He looks hungry." The old woman poured hot tea into three chipped cups and the room was quiet except for Joseph's gentle sucking and Benny's eager slurping.

"Even when there was enough food, he was always hungry." Leah laughed, happy to have something in her belly and a reason to laugh. Then she broached why she had come.

"I have bad news, Freydel. Anna Vashenko was killed the night of the trouble. I brought her satchel of herbs. Please, tell me how each one is used." She emptied the satchel on the long wooden table; its surface nicked by years of cutting and chopping.

"Poor Anna. She was such a loving person. You wish to take Anna's place?" Freydel asked, picking through the dried herbs, heads of flowers, slivers of bark, sniffing some, crumbling others.

"I'm not sure I could," Leah said. "But my husband was murdered that night, so I have to earn money right away. And I worry what happens if my boys get sick." Pointing to the herbs on the table, she asked, "Can you help me?"

"Impossible to learn all in just few minutes." Freydel poked through the herbs, then looked closely at the vials, smelling the potions inside. "These are mostly for pregnant women, to help the sickness in the morning or when the pains start. But I give you some other things, like catnip, hyssop, and licorice root, good for fever or nausea. What can you trade with me?"

"I've brought some potatoes and a little sugar." Leah realized that with so many shortages, the old woman wouldn't be getting many customers from any of the nearby villages for a long time. Still in this time of trouble, she expected that people would share first and ask for payment later. Morris had brought home an endless number of the poor for Sabbath dinner, no matter how near-to- empty their own cupboards were. How many times had she scolded him about those extra mouths to feed, concerned about her own children? Perhaps she was no better than this old woman, who worried about her future.

Freydel wrote down the names of the herbs in Anna's satchel, and added some others, including raspberry leaf, nettle leaves, catnip, bilberry, comfrey as well as ordinary garden ones like garlic, onion, parsley and black walnut hulls, explaining how each could be used. She wrapped each of them in strips of cloth, and put them back in the satchel.

As much as she enjoyed sitting peacefully in a proper home, a fire roaring in the fireplace, Leah knew they had to get home before it got dark. As the late afternoon shadows deepened, she woke the napping Benny, wrapped Joseph in the shawl, tied it around her shoulder and started the long walk to Koritz.

Back in the cellar, she carefully placed the satchel with its precious contents on a high shelf. Her body sagged with fatigue as she sat down on a box. The confines of the cellar felt even smaller, the walls pressing in on her. They couldn't live down here much longer. The damp was dangerous for all of them but especially the baby. Sophia's barn wasn't much better and neither of the houses would be habitable without a lot of rebuilding. And their food supply was disastrously low.

Leah thought about Captain Vaselik's promise of aid for her and Sophia, if they came to his headquarters. Her stomach turned over at the thought of accepting anything from that man, but she had to put her anger aside and think first of the children's welfare. She would force herself to accept Vaselik's paltry offer and get Sophia to come with her. Leah needed to find every bit of food and money she could in order to help them all survive. As a last resort, she would sell the treasures she had buried the night of the attack.

Early the next morning, Leah awoke after another restless night. She had dreamed of Morris, his eyes open and his hands outstretched. She washed her face, trying to wipe away the vision. She fed Benny the bread and milk which she had scrounged yesterday and tried to get Sophia to eat as well, but it was hopeless. The woman still refused to take any nourishment. Nothing could be wasted, so Leah finished it hungrily. Joseph happily nursed, but she worried that her milk might dry up if she didn't get more nourishment.

Vaselik was her only chance. She re-tied her kerchief, smoothed her clothes as much as possible and hoped she looked presentable enough as she and the children left for the headquarters. Sophia was too weak and unable to comprehend anything that Leah said to her, so she stayed in the barn, feet curled up tightly against her chest like a newborn baby.

"Mama, can't I stay here this morning?" Benny pleaded. "I promise to stay close to the cellar." His new shoes had rubbed his feet raw and he complained that he was tired of traipsing after her.

"No. Today I really want you with me." She wrapped Benny's feet in fresh strips of cloth, hoping that the sight of a mother with two hungry children might soften Vaselik's military heart. Even the soldier who dealt Morris that fatal blow had left them unharmed at the last moment. These Russian soldiers were unfathomable.

***

"Captain, there is a woman from the village to see you," Sasha announced to Vaselik as he brought in a tray with the captain's morning tea. It was still early but Vaselik was already in a foul mood. The news that Nicodemus had a cut on his leg had set off his day in the worst possible way. The stable boy had neglected to check the horse before putting him in his stall and now it could be infected. If anything happened to that animal, Vaselik would see to it that the lowly recruit paid dearly and painfully.

"Who is she, what does she want?" Vaselik roared. It irritated him to be constantly bothered by problems from the village, like some local flunky. This recent trouble had made his life impossible with all the complaints he was receiving.

"She says you told her to come, that you had some money and chickens for her."

Vaselik noticed his orderly moving towards the door, as if preparing himself for one of his superior's explosive rages. Such a cowardly little mouse he thought, a real Russian soldier would stand his ground and take it like a man.

Much to Sasha's evident relief, Vaselik smiled, remembering his conversation yesterday with the woman, Leah Peretz. "Yes," he said, "it's alright. Send her in."

Leah entered, holding Joseph against her chest, like a shield between her and Vaselik. Benny peeked shyly around her. But when he saw a shiny sword hanging on the wall, decorated with tassels of red and black, he began to whimper and hid his head in the folds of her skirt.

"What's the matter with the boy?" Vaselik asked.

"That looks like the sword that killed his father," Leah replied coldly.

"Don't be frightened," he said. "I'll put it under the desk, so you won't see it anymore."

Benny stopped crying, but stayed safely behind his mother.

"So you've decided to take my offer," Vaselik said.

"Yes sir," she answered. "Sophia Wolf was too ill to come here today, but since I'm caring for her until she's better, I also ask for her portion."

"What's the problem with her?" Vaselik asked.

"Since the night her husband and son were murdered, she hasn't been able to sleep or eat or even understand anything that is happening. I'm taking care of her, but without our husbands, we're very short of food and money."

Vaselik regarded Leah intently, feeling unexpected compassion for her—he estimated that she was somewhere in her twenties, but these Jews married so young and aged so quickly. Still there was something fierce in her manner which stirred his interest despite his righteous anger towards Jews. Vaselik insisted that the Jewish overseer on his father's estate had cheated his family out of their fortune.

"You need work?" he inquired. "I could use a cook for my men. I'd give you five rubles a month and food for your family."

"Are you serious, Captain? You're not just joking with me?" Tears filled her eyes, but she quickly blinked them away, refusing to let him see her cry.

"Yes, I said so, didn't I?" he answered. He wasn't used to being questioned, certainly not by a woman from the village. "Come tomorrow morning at five o'clock, ready to cook breakfast for thirty soldiers. On the way out, Sasha will give you the chickens and money I promised."

Vaselik was embarrassed by her gratitude and surprised at his own impulse in hiring her. He didn't really need a cook; soldiers were expected to perform jobs like that in the army. And a Jew cooking for Russian soldiers? He had taken such pains to avoid having any Jewish conscripts in his company and now he had just saddled himself with a Jewish cook. Well, if it didn't work, she'd soon be on her way. He had more important things to worry about, like his poor ailing horse.

chapter 5

IT WAS STILL dark when Leah awoke, the cellar quiet except for the steady breathing of Joseph and Benny. She dressed silently, giving the two boys a few more minutes of sleep before waking them, feeling very uneasy about the prospect of her new job. She didn't understand why Captain Vaselik had offered her the chance to earn a little money and some extra food. He hadn't helped anyone else that she knew of, yet here she was preparing to cook for thirty Russian soldiers. Perhaps the very one who had killed Morris.

Benny resisted all efforts to wake him up; but Joseph was content once she offered him a milky breast. There were only a few slices of dried apples and a half cup of milk for Benny's breakfast, but she hoped she could find him something more at the barracks. Aside from cooking breakfast this morning, she wasn't sure what her duties would be, but she assumed that she also would be preparing the soldiers' evening meal. She prayed she'd be permitted to take some food for her children as well. Joseph needed to start on more solid food to supplement his nursing.

Before leaving, Leah also checked on Sophia, who relented and sipped a little milk, but refused anything else. It was impossible to reach her, it was if she were a foreigner and did not understand the language. Leah worried that one day she'd return to find that Sophia had slipped away from this life altogether. The woman was slowly sloughing off all her connections to the world. She seemed resigned to follow her family to the other side.

"Sophia." Leah said gently. "I'm going away for the day but when I return I hope to bring us something good to eat. Please try to get up for awhile, even to just sit and stretch your limbs." Sophia's eyes stayed blank, showing no sign that she understood or cared about anything Leah had to say. "Sophia, you have to try," she insisted, exasperation creeping into her voice. "Just lying there dishonors your husband and your son." Sophia did not even blink in reply.

Leah carried Joseph, pulling the reluctant Benny through the narrow cobblestoned alleyways between rows of houses, moving out of town to the military barracks. In the middle of a large field, next to the stables, was a long, one-storey wooden building. Several horses poked their heads out of their stalls hearing them approach. During the summer, military maneuvers were held in this field, with hundreds of soldiers from regiments all over the province bivouacked there, the smell of cook-fires and horses wafting into town, carried on a warm summer breeze.

Sasha waited outside, his round face ruddy with cold. He ushered her into the attached shed used for cooking, which had a large wood burning stove against one wall and floor to ceiling shelves, crammed with cooking supplies. Through the doorway she saw a room with a long table, benches on either side and a curtain separating the dining area from the place where the men slept.

"We've never had a woman cooking for us," Sasha explained shyly, "so we put up the curtain last night." He pointed out bags of millet, rice, potatoes and semolina which were stacked against the wall. "I already lit the stove and samovar for you."

"Thank you," she said. "What do the men usually have for their morning meal?

"They're not too particular. Kasha or oatmeal, with bread, jam and tea will make them all very happy. If anyone gives you trouble, let me know."

Leah smiled at the thought of this slight, shy man protecting her from any of the more boisterous soldiers, but she thanked him. She found a large basket which would make a comfortable cradle for Joseph and directed Benny to warm himself next to the stove until she could get breakfast underway.

On top of the stove was a large iron kettle, large enough, she thought, for a small child to sleep in, certainly big enough to cook porridge for thirty soldiers.

"Benny, you can help by bringing in the water." She handed the boy two buckets attached to a wooden pole. "But you'll have to make two trips, because I need at least four buckets for the cereal and tea.'

"I'll help him, Missus," Sasha offered. "The well is a bit away from the barracks."

Benny waited for his mother to nod her approval, then slipped on his jacket and a pair of army gloves that Sasha gave him. They were much too big for his small eight-year old hands, but he stood there happily wriggling his fingers inside. After two trips they had drawn enough water and Leah filled the pot, keeping an eye on the samovar and the progress of the fire. She set out thirty bowls, mugs and spoons on the table, hearing the voices of the men on the other side of the curtain, as they dressed, splashed water on their faces, went in and out of the building to the outhouses, then came in to sit quietly at the table waiting for breakfast. Many regarded her with sour expressions, others stopped talking when she came in.

The soldiers lined up, bowls and mugs in hand, to have her portion out the cereal and tea. How strange, she thought, a few nights ago, they might have been the ones who rampaged through her village, now they sat there as quiet as baby lambs. As a child, she had heard horror stories of young Jewish boys, some as young as eight being kidnapped for military conscription, being forced to serve as long as twenty-five years. The length of service was much shorter now, even for Jews. Still, she was sure that Jewish conscripts found life in the military very hard, often brutal.

` Suddenly in the line of soldiers, she saw him. The boy who had killed Morris. The room grew dim and she grabbed the edge of the table to keep from falling. Despite Captain Vaselik's denials, she knew he was Morris's killer. There was no mistake. Her fingers tightened around the knife she held, the urge to plunge it deep into his chest growing inside of her, wanting to strike him the way he had stabbed Morris. Or even screaming for Vaselik, demanding justice. But as her desire for revenge stiffened, she looked across the room at Benny, sitting contentedly eating a crust of dark bread, completely oblivious to the soldier, the first time he had relaxed since the attack. Remarkably, he wasn't frightened by this room full of soldiers. Sasha had been kind to him and he accepted the friendly overtures from some of the other boys. Perhaps it was also the sight of all the good food that was available. He and Joseph were totally dependent on her. How could she jeopardize their welfare by acting rashly? Yet how could she ignore the presence of Morris's murderer, waiting in line for breakfast looking so innocent, big blue eyes in a guileless face?

"Missus, the captain said that he also wants you to cook a hot dinner for the men," Sasha said, interrupting her thoughts. "Please prepare it for five o'clock this evening. Then, you're free to leave. We'll assign someone to serve and clean up after tonight's meal. The captain also said you should take some food for dinner for yourself and the children or you can stay and eat here if you prefer."

She needed this job too desperately to create a commotion at this moment. They also could accuse her of slandering a soldier in the Czar's army. It would be her word against his. She needed to think carefully before she acted. Just bide her time for the moment. The soldier showed no signs of recognizing her, but they hadn't met face-to-face yet.

One teenaged recruit came up, looked in his bowl, then his mug and deliberately spat on the floor, complaining, "This slop is lumpy and the tea looks weak. What the hell is going on?" He was about to throw away the contents of his bowl, when Sasha took his arm and quietly said, "She's here by order of Captain Vaselik. Eat it and be still." Without another word, the boy took his bowl and sat down.

The boy is no more than about sixteen, Leah thought, trying to show off, especially in front of a woman and a Jew besides, someone he thinks is inferior and weak. If he were my son I'd smack some manners into him.

As the next soldier came up to be served, Leah stretched to her full height, looked directly into the boy's eyes while spooning porridge into his bowl, daring him to question her. He looked as if he were about to say something derogatory, but thought better of it and took his bowl and mug and also sat down at his place. By the time it was the turn of the soldier who had stabbed Morris, Leah's expression was rock-hard, ready to fight anyone who might challenge her. The boy simply took his breakfast quietly, completely ignoring Leah. She concentrated on not letting her hands shake, while Benny sat playfully on the sidelines, saluting each soldier who passed by him.

***

Vaselik grunted in irritation as the last soldier left his office. A half dozen of them had tramped in this morning complaining that this Jewess was stealing away their job of cooking. Soldiers expected this opportunity which paid them a few extra kopeks each month and gave them the additional opportunity to pilfer extra rations for themselves. Some military barracks across Russia had mutinied for less, a possibility Vaselik kept in mind every time he issued an order. It was this kind of military insubordination that had begun cropping up that he blamed on Russia's losing the war with the Japanese. Soldiers no longer had the proper respect for authority, unless they had a gun slammed in their faces.

He needed his junior officers to be more effective in keeping things running smoothly, but if he decided to give this Jewess a job, then goddammit, he was in charge. Sniveling boys complaining every time their boots came undone, or their faces needed washing were like buzzing insects that he could swat with just one hand.

Life would have been different if only he had completed the Academy and gotten the posting that he deserved. Once his family lost their land, he could not afford to continue his military studies. Instead, after outstanding service, he was posted in Koritz, where he was required to discipline peasant soldiers, worry about uprisings and pogroms and mollify Jews who constantly complained that they were being persecuted.

He looked at the piles of paperwork that covered his desk. Work orders, money requisitions, supplies to be purchased and inventoried, as if he were some shopkeeper instead of an officer in the Czar's army. And this month he faced his own personal shortages, having lost again at cards. Socializing with the region's gentry meant keeping up appearances, not allowing strangers to know how short of cash he really was.

That evening he stood at his window, watching Leah leave, her baby swaddled in the shawl tied over her shoulder, the boy by her side carrying a basket, no doubt filled with the food Vaselik had authorized. Twilight cast a bluish haze over the icy countryside, and Leah looked like an apparition from another world. He felt again the sting of her anger when she talked about the death of her husband. He usually received more deference from the townspeople, but not this woman whose eyes were like hot coals ready to flare up. These Jews could be so troublesome.

chapter 6

LEAH ENTERED THE cellar, laid Joseph on a soft pile of clothes and looked for a candle stub to light. Benny grew so excited watching his mother unwrap the food that he began jumping in anticipation. He ran in circles around the small space, whooping and hollering, his shadows bouncing against the walls. Even though he had eaten breakfast at the barracks, as well as an afternoon snack, he still stood wide-eyed as Leah brought out four eggs, a loaf of freshly baked bread, a pitcher of milk and some butter.

"Is this all for us, Mama? I'm starving." When she pulled out some cherry preserves from the bottom of the basket, he whooped again. They would be eating well tonight.

"Don't touch anything yet," she said. "I'm going outside to see if I can find a pan and then build a fire."

She smiled at his delight, also happy at the prospect of brewing the pocketful of tea leaves that she had taken. The looters had actually left behind the samovar, so she could make some proper tea tonight. With full bellies, they'd sleep content, despite the chill temperatures. To ward off the constant cold, she had rummaged through the debris of both her house as well as Sophia's place, scouring for any remnants of quilts and blankets that hadn't completely burned. She pieced them together so tonight they would burrow under several layers of clothing and quilts to keep warm.

Like an old miser, Leah kept one of the chickens that Captain Vaselik had given her, hiding it in the loft in Sophia's barn. The other chickens would provide eggs, make a few meals, but with this one she would fatten up and see what she could get in trade. Now with her job as cook, there should be more opportunities for food, maybe even some meat, if only she could convince herself to stay as long as possible. Without a regular *shochet* to kill the animals according to kosher ritual, she knew she was breaking the rules by eating unkoshered meat, but she could only do her best to follow all the traditions.

It was more distressing than she realized to work amongst these soldiers, especially if she had to see that guilty boy everyday. Sometimes she clenched her jaw so tightly that her teeth hurt. But until Holstein's mill was up and running, what else could she do? Surely not even Morris would hold this against her knowing that this job helped his sons survive.

After she fed Benny and nursed Joseph, Leah took a plate of food and a mug of hot tea to Sophia, who remained in the barn. She lay curled under a remnant of a blanket, her face turned to the side. As Leah entered, she looked up weakly, her breath ragged and uneven, sounding raspy, her eyes rheumy and her skin pasty-white as if someone had brushed her face with flour. Sophia made no attempt to eat or even sit up.

"Sophia, this is madness. You must eat." Leah put her arm under her shoulders, trying to raise her up to a sitting position. But Sophia whispered, "Just let me go. Please."

"Nonsense, I'll do nothing of the sort." Leah tried again to raise her up, but Sophia went limp in her arms. Sophia's breath became more ragged, falling to a mere whisper, when Leah heard her exhale in a whooshing sound. Then, there was only silence. Sophia's eyes were open but they stared up lifelessly. Like Morris, her skin had the final sheen of death.

"Oh my god, Sophia, please." Leah called to her, but there was no response. She placed her ear on Sophia's chest, but heard nothing, When she held her hand in front of Sophia's mouth she felt nothing. Once again, someone had died and Leah had been unable to save her.

How was this possible, that this woman had simply willed herself to die? How many times did Leah want to give up, thinking how easy it would be, to simply lay down in a bank of snow and drift off dreaming of food and a warm fire. Life was hard, but she had two children to feed and keep alive. Perhaps that was the reason for Sophia's surrender, she no longer had a family. Nothing could make Leah give up, not the attack, not Morris's death, nor the humiliation of cooking for the soldiers.

Leah remembered another time back in Yanoff, late at night, sitting at the bedside of her mother. By then the cancer had stolen the beauty in her face, the light in her eyes. She liked to have Leah read to her, it helped take her mind off the pain, sometimes even lulled her into sleeping a little.

"Don't forget me, sweetheart." Her mother's voice still had the lilt of a young girl, but one who had become saddened by a great loss. Her lush auburn hair had turned a dull grey framing a face lined by pain and resignation.

"Mama, how silly. You'll be well soon." Her father had said so and he wouldn't lie to her, pretend if it wasn't true. Leah wanted to believe him with every inch of her fourteen year old body, but the expression on his face told her otherwise.

"Take care of Papa, keep him from being too lonely." Her mother weakly raised her hand, one finger beckoned Leah closer. "You mustn't mourn me, my love." And then she closed her eyes, took a last breath and was gone.

The first to die that Leah couldn't save. No power over life and death.

"Leah," a voice called out in the dark, bringing Leah back to the present. "It's me, Gittel."

"In here, Gittel, in the barn." Gittel peered in and stopped short when she saw Sophia lying there. "Benny told me you were here. How is she doing?" she asked quietly.

"Sophia died a few minutes ago," Leah said, reaching over to close the vacant eyes staring ahead.

"Oh my God," Gittel gasped, putting her hands over her face. "Was she sick?"

"Just sick of life," Leah answered. "Without Abraham or Isaac, she didn't know how to survive. She refused to eat or get up. Then tonight, she just died."

"Too much sorrow these days." Gittel said. She bent down and covered the body with the blanket. "Are you alright?"

"Just tired, Gittel. Very tired." Leah rested against the stall, noticing Gittel regarding the plate of food, which lay untouched next to Sophia. She was a big woman, once oversized, but now Leah realized, much thinner, her face more gaunt.

"Please, take this," Leah offered. "I hate to see it go to waste." There was a moment's hesitation and she saw how embarrassed Gittel felt as she reached over and began eating quickly before the offer was rescinded.

"Today, I started to cook for Captain Vaselik's regiment," Leah said, "so that may help a little."

"How can you work for that man, Leah?" Gittel finished eating and color returned to her face. "He did nothing to stop the trouble."

"Those were eggs I took from the army kitchen that you just wolfed down," Leah said, an angry flush coloring her own cheeks. "I'll do any honest work for anyone, the Czar himself, if it keeps my babies fed and warm."

"People are not going to understand, Leah."

"People, Gittel? Or you?" Leah was standing eye-to-eye with Gittel. " If I want to share my goods with you or other people, will you refuse? Should I let my children starve?"

Gittel turned to leave. Leah shouted after her, "Shame on you! Each day I face soldiers who hate me and now my neighbor, too?"

Leah looked down at Sophia. "Maybe you're the lucky one. Sleep in peace, my friend."

How could Gittel turn on her that way? She had been the friend who brought food when Rachel had died and Leah was unable to rise from her bed to cook or care for Morris. Gittel was the neighbor who rejoiced with her when Benny, her first healthy child was born. Leah sat up with Gittel when her boy Yussel had fallen and broken his arm. They were neighbors.

There was no restful sleep for Leah that night. She knew that early in the morning before she started cooking breakfast for the soldiers, she would have to bury Sophia by herself, unless she found someone to help her. She hoped to manage without Benny, so the boy would not have to face yet another death.

Everyday the boy took his prayer book and recited Kaddish, the prayer for the dead, to honor Morris, his eight-year-old face so grave as he said the words. Every Jewish father prayed to have a son to carry on his name, to recite Kaddish at his death, to fulfill the Commandments. Morris had taught Benny well.

Leah's night was roiled by dreams of faces looming over her as she tried to make her way through a dark thicket. Morris appeared, his beard smeared with blood, his lips silently moving as she strained to hear what he was saying. Sophia and her family followed after him, their eyes blank, mouths a thin grim line. But the most frightening was the face of the young soldier, holding her silver and tortoise-shell combs and laughing, his fingers caressing them as if they were flesh and blood. Leah screamed for her brothers and her father to help her, when she was suddenly awakened by the baby crying. She sat up, not sure whether she too had cried out, but Benny still slept undisturbed, not bothered for once by his own nightmares.

She reached for Joseph, held him close to her, nursing him, his baby smells sweet and milky, the sounds of his sucking, regular and comforting. In the dark quiet of the cellar, she thought about the other babies, the one she held so briefly, but loved no less. Little dark-haired Rachel, her first-born, the daughter who never lived long enough to have an official naming ceremony.

"That's alright, my sweet," Leah whispered. "We made our own ceremony, didn't we?"

She held her own personal ritual in those last moments before the baby died, reciting prayers and officially giving the baby the name of Rachel, after her mother.

If she had been the one killed and Morris was left, he would have chalked it all up to the mysteries of the Divine, in the same way he found comfort when Rachel died, or at the death of the two still-born girls. After each death, he endured her raging, then retreated into his prayer books to seek the solace that was denied to her.

"It was God's will," he repeated each time, not knowing how to comfort her or help her stop crying. "I don't want any part of your God," she stormed at him, knowing that this would hurt him almost as much as the death did.

Ironically, she thought, it was his religious and scholarly side that had made him such a catch as a husband. With only a small dowry, she would never have been matched with a major scholar, but Fannie the matchmaker said Morris didn't care about money, didn't even care about *kest*, the tradition of a groom living with and being supported by the bride's family for the first year. And naive girl that she was, she remembered how excited she was at the prospect of moving to a new place, starting her own home with her own husband.

Her childhood in Yanov seemed more like a dream than ever, their modest house filled with books, all of them available to Leah, no restrictions on her learning anything that spurred her curiosity. Her father and two brothers doted on her, spoiling her with their love, trying to make up for the illness and death of her mother.

She looked down at Joseph still hungrily nursing, as she transferred him to the other breast, his eyes closing, fighting sleep so he could continue feeding. His skin felt strangely warm to her considering the chilled temperatures in the cellar. The silky hairs on the top of his head were damp with perspiration, yet he nursed contentedly. She was becoming alarmed for no reason, too easily agitated, she thought, exacerbated by all the daily problems. If she could have even one good night's sleep, she'd be able to manage her days more calmly.

Leah automatically awoke at the first light of dawn. She and Joseph had both dozed sitting bundled together. She was so exhausted that as much as she regretted it, it would be necessary to have Benny's help to bury Sophia. Children in this *shtetl*, like Benny, were growing up too quickly, with no childhood to fall back on. She splashed water on her face from the jug, put a clean cloth around Joseph, who whimpered a little at being touched. Benny, however, resisted all entreaties to get up.

"I know, it's a hard way to start the day, but Mama needs you." He rose grumpily, washed his face, then swallowed some milk flavored with a spoonful of the cherry preserves and followed Leah out into the brisk morning air.

"Let's hope this is the last of these duties we'll ever have to perform," Leah said, gently lifting Sophia's body onto the cart for the trip to the cemetery. The woman weighed so little, it felt as if a stiff breeze could blow her away like dandelion fuzz before they laid her into the ground. As she had done with the other grave sites, Leah marked a piece of wood with Sophia's name, date of death, declaring her to be a good and loving wife and mother. Benny recited the Kaddish and they left for the barracks. Another day had begun.

chapter 7

IT WAS EARLY morning and Leah was ready to leave for the barracks, when she heard a horse neighing outside. Still alarmed by unexpected noises, she cautiously peeked out through a crack in the door and saw the familiar horse and wagon of old Peddler Foreman. But instead of the old man, a much younger man sat up on the seat behind Drushka, the old man's horse, steam puffing out of the animal's nostrils. The young man was dressed shabbily, a wool cap pulled low over his eyes, a thin jacket offering little protection from the frosty air.

"Hey," she called. "Where's Peddler Foreman?"

No one knew exactly how old the peddler was, but she fondly remembered his monthly visits, arriving no matter what the weather or the condition of the roads, his wagon piled high with all sorts of useful items, pots and pans, needles, scissors for sewing, reams of cloth, seeds for planting, tools, used clothing and most important of all, news of the region. He would trade or barter if you did not have money and eagerly shared the latest gossip.

"I'm his grandson, Yaakov," the young man said. "My grandfather isn't well so I'm doing his route. Anything you need today?"

Leah laughed. "Yes, a whole new house would be nice. What do you have in small wooden shacks?"

"We heard about the attack. Looks like everyone will be needing things," he said with a serious expression. "I can bring you building supplies next time if you need them."

"Come in for a cup of hot tea," Leah said. "I have to leave for work, but you look frozen."

Yaakov shot her a grateful look and scrambled down quickly. He followed her into the cellar, trying not to bump his head on the doorway. "My grandfather speaks of you very warmly. I know he misses his visits very much."

"Send him my best regards," she said. "Still he must be glad he doesn't have to deal with all this death and destruction."

"Things are so bad here, I'll be returning as often as I can." He pushed his cap further back on his head, checking out the cramped living space.

"What could you trade today for a very plump chicken?" she asked eagerly, motioning him conspiratorially to follow her, a finger on her lips to keep him silent.

They went into the Wolfs' barn, and Leah climbed up to the loft and brought down the hidden chicken, in its crate, pecking away at the grains that Leah had fed it.

"I need something really worthwhile in exchange."

"You're very lucky to still have a chicken left." Yaakov said. "If you can wait until I come back next week, I'll bring vegetables. Also some salt, and maybe even some meat."

Leah's face burned, even though Yaakov had no idea how she managed to get this chicken. Why feel guilty? Wasn't losing a husband a steep enough price to pay for a chicken and a few kopeks?

"Maybe you could also bring me some mugs and plates and an iron skillet." She tried not to sound too greedy. "The bird has been nicely fattened up, so she's certainly worth it."

"Anything else to trade?" Yaakov peered around, to see what was available.

"This was my neighbor's barn," she answered. "I don't feel right taking their things. Besides after the looters, there probably isn't much left."

"I'll see what I can round up for you on my next trip. I'll be back in a week."

"If you don't mind, I'll hold onto the chicken until you come back," she said. No one was getting this bird before she got full payment.

As Yaakov drove away, Leah realized that she hadn't asked him for any news or tidbits of gossip. That used to be the best part of his grandfather's stop. She would offer the old man a glass of hot tea and a slice of bread and jam, and in return he gave her a glimpse of the outside world. This young man was all business, not even a smile.

***

The only advantage that Ivan Vaselik enjoyed as captain of his regiment was the allotment which allowed him to live in the house of the Widow Popov, instead of at the barracks. He rented her former bedroom which had two windows overlooking an unkempt garden, shaded by a large oak tree. The widow prepared a plate of cold meat and pickled cucumbers in summer or a bowl of hot soup and fresh bread in winter, leaving it each night, along with a small carafe of vodka. He had to firmly entreat her not to fuss so much over him, because in exchange for her care, she thought it entitled her to monitor his comings and goings, poking her head out every time she heard the front door open or shut. Since she did not have any other family living at home, she treated him as an honored relative, which he found stifling .

Lately he began going to his office early every day, enjoying the morning meals that the woman, Leah Peretz, cooked for the soldiers. Oatmeal clotted with heavy cream or sprinkled with coarse dark sugar or thin blinis filled with fruit preserves, instead of the overcooked boiled eggs the Widow Popov served, along with her tedious and boring conversation.

The men in the company, of course, wolfed down their food without a word of thanks, nurturing their anger at being denied the opportunity of cooking, which also meant they couldn't also take supplies and sell them outside the camp. Everyday someone came to his office to complain that they were sure that the "Jewess" was stealing. They all knew it wasn't true, but there didn't seem to be any way of stopping the discontentment. He relied on Sasha to alert him to any action that might turn mutinous, otherwise Vasalik ignored it as the usual grumbling of restless, ill-paid soldiers.

In addition to watching Leah's departure each day, he often stood at his window as she arrived in the morning, both children in tow as usual.

He never saw her smile, but she never complained either. She focused on her work and her boys. He wondered what her life had been like before coming to Koritz. Her bearing spoke of a different sort of upbringing from some of the other villagers. Before the attack, he sometimes saw her at the market, carrying a basket of vegetables for sale, sometimes accompanied by her husband, who always looked distracted. Because of his dealings with them in the village and contact with those in the army, Vaselik felt he was an expert on the subject of Jews. Always angry, always petitioning that they had been unfairly conscripted, stubbornly refusing to convert to Russian Orthodoxy, even when the military tried to force them. Russian state newspapers reported stories about their deficiencies, their differences from full-blooded Russians, egging on the Russians' hatred of Jews. They were a stiff-necked people he decided and he had nothing in common with them. The ones he met had no interest in any of his pleasures: gambling, horses or beautiful women. And there was always the matter of his family's estate, looming in the back of his mind, confirming his conviction that his father had been cheated by his Jewish overseer. Still this woman was different. He sensed she also had a stubborn, rebellious streak, but he would bet that it had nothing to do with her religion.

"Sasha," he called. "Tell the Peretz woman to come here."

A few minutes later, Leah appeared at the office doorway. "Yes, Captain. You wanted to see me?"

"Next week some of my army colleagues will be visiting and I am going to host a dinner for them. I'd like you to cook and serve that night."

"Would there be extra payment for my services, Captain?" Leah tried not to appear too eager, but she was already thinking of what she could buy with the additional wages.

"Is money all you Jews ever think about?" Vaselik asked. "Do you never think of anything else?"

"It's easy to be so offhand about money when you have it," she replied coldly. "I need to worry about my children's survival. If you were a parent, you would understand."

So, he thought, you just need to provoke her to get a show of emotion. This was the first time that she had displayed any since she spoke of her husband's death. Usually she was so careful to appear unemotional, almost stoic. But now her eyes had a flash of fire back in them. He couldn't help thinking that dressed and fed properly, she would be a handsome woman, not beautiful, but attractive.

"Wait," he said, seeing she was turning to leave. "Of course you would be paid for your time. I'm not an unreasonable man."

"Thank you Captain. I'd be happy to help."

chapter 8

LEAH KNOCKED ON the door of the Widow Popov's house, accompanied as always by Benny and Joseph. The baby squirmed in her arms, while Benny looked curiously at the big wooden door with the lion's head knocker. The door opened slightly and a woman's voice said, "Go to the back door, where the kitchen is." Then the door slammed shut .

She remembered the Popov woman from market days, her round face sniffing snobbishly at the wares other women sold, always picking through the vegetables, always haggling unpleasantly over the price. Leah appreciated a negotiation, bargaining was part of the game, but what she could not forgive was the widow's pleasure in humiliating others by making the insults personal. Before her husband died, the Widow Popov was considered to be the prosperous wife of a local tavern owner, who also invested in another drinking establishment in the nearby town of Fastov. But one morning while shaving, he keeled over, dead before he hit the floor. It was then that Irene Popov discovered piles of unpaid bills and gambling debts and before the funeral supper was eaten, an angry group of creditors was banging on her door. Now she was simply the Widow Popov, forced to rent out her own bedroom in order to put food on her table and to keep from being one of the homeless poor.

Leah didn't think that the woman's unfortunate circumstances had done anything to improve her manner, if possible, she had become nastier. Leah could understand that adversity didn't necessarily make a person more pleasant. She was also angry at the world, but there would be no sharing confidences between the two ladies. Not with the Widow Popov, who continued to treat Leah like a servant and potential thief.

Leah placed Joseph in a basket on a chair in the corner near the stove, gave him a piece of cloth soaked in sugar water to suck on until he dozed off. Benny sat next to him reading one of Morris's favorite prayer books. It was a small book, its cover stained with blotches of red, but the boy insisted on keeping it with him at all times, tucked inside his shirt. Now he slowly recited the words he recognized, just as his father had taught him.

"This is the food for Captain Vasalik's dinner tonight." Widow Popov stood over Leah, like a large bull, filling up the space, pointing to the supplies that Vaselik had sent in. "Be sure you don't touch anything else. Understand?"

Leah stared back defiantly. The woman dressed all in black taffeta as might befit a prosperous widow, but the collar was worn and the cuffs a bit threadbare, so probably this dress was from better days, worn just to demonstrate that she was the woman of the house and Leah just an interloper, not deserving of any courtesy.

Tonight Vaselik was hosting a dinner for three officers who were friends from the army. He had approved a menu of roast chicken stuffed with prunes, kasha with mushrooms, roasted potatoes and baked apples with cinnamon and to start the evening, salted herring and vodka. She couldn't remember when she had seen such a feast even before the attack. With this menu she would not have to cook meat and dairy together. Adhering to kosher rules was second nature to Leah, learning it first at home with her parents and then keeping kosher during her marriage to Morris. As rebellious as she was, there were some rituals it never occurred to her to flout. That included the kosher ritual of keeping dairy and meat separate, not eating animals with cloven hooves and the special way of killing the animal. These rules she observed.

The cuisine at the barracks was very basic, even though she tried to add some refinement to her dishes. Tonight was a unique opportunity to use the cooking skills she had learned from her mother, in the days before she became so sick. It was an opportunity for Leah to shine before the four officers.

It was exhilarating at being in a proper kitchen again, even with the Widow eyeing her suspiciously and constantly checking that she didn't pocket even a crust of bread. Benny sat contentedly next to the oven, feeling its heat seep in like old memories of happier days when he would lie on the shelf above their stove keeping warm. He used a piece of burnt wood on a scrap of paper to practice copying words from the prayer book, while Joseph sat propped up in his basket, peeking over the edge.

Since it was Saturday, Leah did not start her preparations until after sundown. This was the only day she refused to cook for the soldiers. Vaselik had grumbled but finally agreed that her job would be six days a week, with Saturday off until dark. Friday afternoon she would leave an evening meal warming for the soldiers, just as she used to do for her own family, so there would be no cooking once *Shabbos* started.

Pungent odors filled the kitchen and Leah let herself pretend that this was her place and the people arriving in the next room were her guests. The officers sounded jovial at first, becoming more raucous as they burst into song, Vaselik's strong baritone leading the way. This male presence made her think of the days she spent growing up with her two brothers and their father. She had loved the teasing and bantering with Dov and Simon which continued even after her mother grew sick. As the only girl, her father made her feel special trying to soften the sometimes sad sickroom atmosphere in the house. Tonight the men's voices grew so loud that it took no effort to overhear their stories recounting army life and the tales of all the women's hearts they had so carelessly broken.

Leah peered through the open kitchen door to get a glimpse of the three guests. They were not dressed in uniform, but in loose fitting tops, their pants tucked into knee-high boots. It was the first time that she had seen Vaselik out of uniform, his flushed cheeks no doubt due to the shots of vodka that were being downed in quick succession. His eyes seemed to light up reflecting the comradeship he was enjoying, away from the hassles of command. He had relaxed the strict military martinet side that was always on display.

She had expected to leave once the food was prepared and the main course served, but the captain seemed determined to show off to his friends how important he was, by having not only the Widow Popov in attendance, but his own personal cook ready to serve.

Earlier, he complained about her shabby clothes, the bits and remnants she managed to piece together that hadn't been looted or ruined by the attackers, insisting that she wear a dress which Sasha delivered to her.

"I won't be shamed in front of my friends, with you looking as if I had pulled you in off the street," he said, circling around, checking the effect of the dress, as if he were choosing a fat pullet at market.

"Must you keep your head covered with that rag of yours?" he asked, making a face at the kerchief which was always tied around her hair.

"You know perfectly well, Captain, that the hair of a Jewish married woman can only be seen by her husband, otherwise it must be covered or she wears a wig." It was humiliating enough to be wearing a uniform like a servant, without being insulted. She focused very hard on the extra rubles she was earning, in order to keep quiet.

"I've seen those wigs on some of the more affluent Jewish women,' he said. "Better they went about bald than wearing those ugly pieces, which look as if a bird had nested on their heads. Alright keep the kerchief, but I insist you wear this dress."

It was a modest grey woolen dress with long sleeves, edged in white lace at the cuffs and collar. Since it wasn't hers to keep and she was wearing it for only one night, where no one but these strangers would see her, it was less of a problem to agree than argue with the captain. She couldn't help noticing a jealous look in Irene Popov's eyes when she saw Leah in the dress, which continued to delight Leah as she prepared dinner. Serves the old witch right.

**

Vaselik wanted this evening to be perfect. His guests were old army buddies, old friends since their days as young cadets at the same military academy. Although he was forced to leave when his family's money was lost, their continued friendship made his transition tolerable. At the Academy, they had protected each other; if one was late in returning from leave or was in danger of being discovered while drunk. Vaselik had even successfully answered for Mikhail one morning at roll call, when his friend didn't make it back in time.

Now the big news was that Dmitry Bukolov was in line to become a member of the Royal Guard. During the war with Japan, Bukolov had a brief moment of glory holding off a Japanese advance and his family had parlayed that to get him a more advantageous posting. It was painful for Vaselik to remember how he had always been the bright shining star during those early years. Everyone in his class assumed that Ivan Vaselik would be the war hero, receive a royal commission, or at the very least, marry into riches. But nothing like that happened. He was acknowledged as a first rate officer, but with no family financial backing, he never had enough grease to keep the wheels of his career moving. Life had become like an unending game of cards, constantly bluffing everyone into believing that his hand was superior to theirs, that he was only one card away from winning the entire pot. Pretending all the time was tiresome and exhausting but preferable to having others know the truth.

It was important to impress his guests tonight, so he bought the finest vodka, the best salted herring, special little grape and walnut candies, hired the Peretz woman to cook and serve and permitted the Widow Popov to flutter about, treating him as if he were the Czar himself.

During the evening, Vaselik wasn't sure if Bukolov, Diemchuk, and Katko were really fooled as he watched them through a thickening haze of vodka and Turkish cigarettes. He noticed how too much alcohol and too many late nights had left Mikhail Katko's face puffy like rising dough, while Andre Diemchuk now had deepening lines of bitterness encircling his eyes. Only Dmitry sat smugly self-satisfied, contemplating his future reward at Court. After they had gulped down a few more glasses of vodka, Vaselik began to believe that his own fortunes could change again.

"Ivan, what ever happened to that woman whom you wooed all during training?" Andre Diemchuk asked. "Did you ever bed her?"

"What eyes she had," said Mikhail. "And hips that invited immediate conquest." He twirled his moustaches and licked his lips, imitating a villain from a cheap melodrama.

Vaselik laughed, but said nothing. She had been an early love, bedeviling him with her flirtatious ways, using her husband, Vaselik's superior officer, as a shield of virtue if men tried to get too close. But Vaselik had overcome her defenses, whispering promises of undying love, gifting her with flowers and gold bracelets. If they had been discovered, his life literally would have been over, never mind his military career. Her husband had never lost a duel. Even now, Vaselik felt nervous twinges admitting to the liaison, knowing that her husband was still a favorite at Court. But, he grew warm remembering their last rendezvous, thinking of the porcelain whiteness of her breasts pressed against his chest, her mouth pinned to his, both of them ignoring the danger in their dalliance.

"Love is very fleeting when you're in the military," Vaselik said sharply. "A quick kiss, a warm bed, hello, goodbye, that's all you have time for."

"Especially if the lady's husband is so good with a pistol," Dmitry laughed. "You were one lucky man."

The four of them reminisced at having been the most notorious cadets in their regiment in capturing any woman's heart they focused on. They would sweep into a café, buys drinks for everyone, dance all night with the slightly shady ladies and exit again, unscathed, untouched by any real emotion. But among the four, Vaselik had been the undisputed king of the flirtations. He was taller, hair thicker, moustaches fuller, eyes darker, but he never allowed his heart to become involved.

Leah entered, carrying a large steaming platter of chicken, fragrant with prune stuffing, surrounded by roasted potatoes. "I'll bring the rest of the food," she said, blushing under the stares of the four men.

Vaselik noted how pink her cheeks were, how different she looked dressed properly, even with that blasted kerchief around her head. One mischievous curl had slipped out from the scarf, its deep auburn color unexpected and startling against the pale luminescence of her skin. The other three officers sat up straighter in their chairs, looking less drunk than they had appeared before.

"Don't get any ideas," he said when she had left the room. "She's a widowed Jew and my cook, so forget whatever you're thinking."

"And you Ivan, what are you thinking?" asked Mikhail. "Less risk than a superior's wife, no?"

"Nonsense. You know how I feel about Jews. They destroyed my family and made my life impossible."

"We know, we've heard the story of how the overseer swindled your father and ruined him. All the more reason to get your revenge." Andre snorted as he finished his vodka in one swallow. The other two followed suit, but Vaselik said nothing. He saw only Leah's pale skin set off by that one teasing bright curl.

chapter 9

EARLY THE NEXT morning, Leah was already at work at the barracks kitchen when Sasha walked in with a parcel wrapped in newspaper, tucked under his arm.

"This is for you, ma'am," he said, his voice barely a whisper, avoiding looking directly at Leah as he thrust the package towards her. "It's from the captain. He said you left it at the Widow Popov's."

She was in the midst of stirring a huge pot of oatmeal and although she was very curious, she delayed opening it until everyone had been served and she had finished brewing the tea. All through her chores, her attention remained focused on the package stowed on a shelf above the sink.

Leah noted that many of the soldiers remained seated at the tables, intently watching as she peeled away a corner of the newspaper and saw a bit of grey material of the dress she had worn last night peeking out. She re-wrapped it and turned away so that Sasha and the soldiers couldn't see her blushing. Vaselik knew she didn't want the dress, that it would be improper to accept a present from him. The dilemma was how to return it without making him angry.

Leah had hoped to receive some response from her brothers and father to her letter asking for financial help. It was the first time she had permitted herself to ask her family for aid. All during her marriage, she had kept up the pretense that everything was fine. The long distance didn't allow for many visits so her secret had been safe. Now she needed help urgently.

As she collected empty bowls from the tables, Leah worried that she hadn't heard from them. If they could help ease her situation until Holstein's mill was running again, she wouldn't have to be so dependent on this army job.

More annoyingly, there was the reaction of some of her neighbors. Since working for the captain, a few, especially Gittel, barely acknowledged her when they passed each other in town. Benny had come home in tears last Saturday, after one of his friends refused to play with him, yelling his mother was a traitor. Everyone in the village did business with the soldiers, why had she suddenly become such a pariah?

Leah dried his tears and sat Benny in the light under the slit of the cellar window. He turned away to study the Saturday prayers, pretending that he didn't care.

"Benny, I know that some of the neighbors don't like my working for the soldiers." She made him turn around to face her. "I'm sorry the children are being mean to you, but I'm not doing anything wrong. I need to earn money for us." He ignored her and continued his studies, but she saw that his eyes were too full of tears to read. "You like Sasha. Hasn't he been a good friend to you?"

Now she stacked the dirty dishes in a large vat of heated water. Rivulets of perspiration dripped down the back of her neck as she leaned over the rising steam. Her work had begun to redden her hands and being in hot water so much of the day, they had begun to crack and bleed. Even during the hardest times of her marriage, she had kept her hands soft by rubbing them with chicken grease, but nothing protected them now. She feared she was starting to look like an aging babushka, those grandmotherly types who cared nothing about their appearance. Her mother even at her most ill, insisted on being groomed and brushed. Her father had protested that it didn't matter under the circumstances, but Leah knew that he had always thought her mother beautiful and her mother wanted to stay beautiful in his eyes.

She went over everything in her head. As she dried the clean bowls and placed them on the shelf, she asked herself what other choice did she have? Without this job her family would go hungry. The charity groups in the shtetl had very little money to spare and it didn't seem right to take money if she could earn some honestly. Her worst problem was being in the same room with the soldier she knew was Morris's killer. Seeing him galled her every time he passed, his baby face looking so innocent. Every time she saw him eating breakfast, laughing with his buddies, she had to restrain herself from stabbing him or throwing a pot of boiling water at him. Even now her fantasy of killing was so real, she actually saw his face contort in pain, heard him gasping as his breath grew short. She was so completely focused on her revenge that she didn't see Sasha come in with the captain's breakfast tray.

"Are you alright, Missus?" Sasha asked, looking worried. "Why don't you go outside for some fresh air? I'll get one of the boys to collect the rest of the bowls."

First, she checked to make sure that Joseph was alright in the corner playing with a strand of wooden beads that one of the soldiers had carved for him. Some of the boys had adopted Joseph as their little mascot, making toys or giving him special tidbits of food. And Sasha had taken a strong liking to Benny, so Leah often found extra cookies or candies in the basket of food she took home. It was Leah who was the object of the soldiers' disdain. They muttered behind her back, making sure that she heard every complaint they said. "Jewish whore" was their favorite epithet.

Outside a light dusting of snow covered the ground like powdered sugar. The cold air chilled her but cleared her head of her murderous thoughts. No matter what the difficulties, she had to continue to work here until she saved enough money. There was a house to rebuild and Benny needed to go back to school when it reopened. She would find a way to deal with Captain Vaselik as diplomatically as possible.

After everything had been cleared away from the tables and she had swept the dining area, Leah instructed Benny to stay in the kitchen and watch Joseph, while she took the dress, still wrapped in the parcel, and knocked on the Captain's door. Before Sasha could stop her, she went right into the office.

"Captain, could I have a word with you?" She stood in the doorway, barring Sasha from entering.

"Yes, what is it?" Vaselik sat at his desk, his back to the door, staring off into empty space.

"Sir, I appreciate your giving me the opportunity to cook last night, but please, Captain, I cannot keep the dress." She reached over and placed the package on his desk.

"Dammit, what is this big concern about dresses? I want you to wear it anytime you cook for me. It's not a personal present." He threw it back at her with such force that the paper tore open and the dress fell to the floor.

Leah bent down to pick it up, but as she did she noticed some items on the desk. She gasped when she saw a pair of tortoise shell combs, layered with silver.

Her chest constricted, a cry rose and exploded from the back of her throat. "Where did you get these?"

"What business is it of yours?" He was mortified that any of the spoils from the attack were found in his possession when he was supposed to be the village's protector.

Leah stood, her mouth tasting of dust, her eyes blurred by tears, reliving that awful night as she handed the young soldier her precious combs. "Those combs belonged to my mother and her mother before her," she wept. "I gave them to a soldier to keep him from killing my children."

Her words were weapons fired at Vaselik. She screamed louder, "How did you get them?" not caring whether her voice pierced the walls or if anyone outside the office heard her.

Vaselik flushed scarlet, his eyes glued to her face, but said nothing. Finally, he took the combs and pressed them into her hands, then bolted out of the office, leaving Leah doubled over, clutching the combs tightly. He fled quickly to the stables where Nicodemus was saddled and ready for their morning ride. He mounted, digging his heels deep into the horse's flanks, urging him faster and faster into a wild gallop, racing through the village, shouting for everyone to get out of his way, scattering villagers who were at risk of being run down by a madman and his horse.

He had allowed that woman to get under his skin, been upset by her crying over her damned combs. He was in charge of a barracks in the middle of nowhere, filled with disgruntled soldiers, a situation simmering with danger, which at any moment might flare up in mutiny. What did he care about this woman and her problems? But the image of those dark eyes filled by tears, her body crumpled in grief, thoroughly shamed him.

He immediately thought of his beautiful mother dressing for one of her frequent parties, dark shiny hair piled high on her head, fastened with silver combs. She hated living away in the country and used any excuse to return to Moscow's social scene, even though his father, who could deny her nothing, accompanied her less and less often.

Her laugh sparkled like delicate crystal, as she called out to him, "Vanya, my pet, Mama is leaving now. Come give me a kiss goodnight."

Once again he felt the velvet of her dress against his cheek, her gardenia scent filling his nostrils.

Vaselik flew by a trio of villagers on the side of the road, who tried to wave him down, but he had no time or patience to stop and hear more troubles this morning. As the image of his mother faded he saw his father sprawled on the floor, a gun clenched in his hand, blood pooling around his face, while his mother stood in the doorway screaming.

He was sick of all these problems from constantly complaining Jews. Enough too, of this woman. She can't stay at this job any longer.

As soon as Vaselik returned to camp, he called Sasha into his office. "This Peretz woman," he snapped, "get rid of her. I don't want to see her here again." He pretended to busy himself shuffling papers waiting for Sasha to obey his order.

"Did you hear me, or do I have to beat you a little to improve your hearing?" Vaselik yelled. Has everyone gone mad? "Don't stand there, go do as I said."

Sasha found Leah peeling potatoes for the evening meal. Her shoulders sagged as she methodically picked up each potato, sliced off the skin and put it in a big pot of water. Her eyes were swollen from crying.

"I'm sorry, Missus," Sasha said slowly, spitting out the words with great difficulty. "The captain has decided he doesn't need a cook after all. I'm to give you your wages and a big bag of food for you to take with you."

"What?" At first she couldn't understand what this little man was saying. Not work here? Just when she had convinced herself against all reason to stay. The captain was firing her? "Who will finish tonight's meal?"

"Don't you worry. I'll get one of the soldiers who cooked before to take over."

He turned to Benny, who sat nearby, frightened by his mother's expression. "And you young lad, I have something that I made especially for you." From his pocket, Sasha pulled out three wooden soldiers, intricately carved and dressed in the uniforms of a private, a Cossack and a general. "These are souvenirs from your friend Sasha."

Benny took them and mumbled a shy "Thank you."

"No, give it back," she barked. To Leah this was the last straw, a Russian soldier giving her boy a remembrance, of what, their cruelty, their looting? Benny looked so disappointed that she had to relent, despite her distaste, not having the heart to deny him anything that might give him even one second of pleasure. "It's alright, you can take it."

She folded her apron, gathered her things and picked up Joseph, while Sasha packed a basket of food for them to take home. All her best efforts to keep this job, all for nothing. No matter how hard she tried, she was failing.

When Leah's mother died and she was completely in charge of the household, she was fourteen years old. She felt decades older, after having tended to her mother in her illness and running everything by herself, even under her mother's tutelage. She knew she had lived a charmed childhood up to then, limited only by her own curiosity and dreams. Books came right after food in importance, certainly for Leah, more than religious practice.

Her father was observant, but somewhat from duty, like Leah, he had his favorite practices and followed those more carefully than some of the others.

"Observing the Sabbath," he had confided to her, "is my favorite, because since we're not allowed to work, we can take our books and read all day down by the river." It was their special time, an afternoon under the shade of an apple tree, overlooking the Pripyat.

Keeping kosher was a given. If you lived among Jews, there was no other way of eating and cooking. Leah never expected lightning to strike her if she disobeyed any of the tenets, but since most Jews lived close together in neighborhoods, no one dared to be different.

The characters in her favorite Russian novels were all high society or horribly poor, flouting the rules or else hemmed in and stifled by them. Given a choice, Leah favored the former. She always assumed that she would marry and raise a family, but she still dreamt that she would find a great love, just like her parents did. Their union might have been arranged, but her father and mother met as chlildren and knew long ago that they were *beshert*, destined for each other.

Her life with Morris was a big disappointment, when she learned that life and love did not always go together. Having a small dowry limited her opportunities, but her father was most concerned that her husband would be a learned man, a decent human being, someone who would treat her with care. In that respect, Morris was the perfect candidate. He too was looking for the right mate, a woman who was not concerned with material goods, a hard worker who could keep a Jewish home. She filled the bill, young and strong, with the makings of a good homemaker. But her marriage was not like the shining example of her parents and disappointment made her tongue sharper than it had ever been before. Every little thing seemed to loom large and insurmountable.

"In Judaism," she pointed out cuttingly to Morris, "a husband is supposed to treat his wife like a precious jewel and use Shabbos as a time of lovemaking."

Morris always blushed in embarrassment whenever she brought up anything intimate. "A wife is not supposed to belittle her husband, he is the head of the household." That was his final retort before going back to his studies.

Without the bond of love, which was supposed to grow between them, she felt alone and deprived. Instinctively her fingers moving slowly inside her had brought her some relief, but no pleasure.

Still, Morris at the end, thought only of his family. Leah regretted all the times she had berated him for things he could not control. She wished she had shown him greater tenderness.

chapter 10

"MAMA, WAKE UP. Someone is banging on the door."

Benny shook Leah's shoulder to wake her. She opened her eyes to see terror on the boy's face. Now that she wasn't cooking for the soldiers, she slept a little later instead of rising at the first trace of dawn, but this morning the sound of knocking had entered the dream she was having. She encountered Morris again, this time looking angry and banging his fist. The knocking at the door woke Joseph, who cried and demanded to be changed and fed. In their small cellar space, all occurrences no matter how ordinary, became dramatic and chaotic.

"It's alright, Benny." She got up, wrapped a shawl around her shoulders, adjusted her kerchief, and called through the door, "Who is it?"

"It's Yaakov, ma'am, Peddler Foreman's grandson."

Leah opened the door to find the young man standing there, a large bundle slung over his shoulder. It was barely light, but she heard her neighbors stirring a few doors down. Yaakov's cap covered his ears, but his face was turning red from the cold.

"I have the things you asked for, Mrs. Peretz. Also, my grandfather sends his regards and a new book as a present for you."

"Ahh, Yaakov. Things have changed since you were here last time. I've lost my job and can't afford to pay you. Now I have to save every kopek for food." She looked longingly at the pots and tools poking out of the bundle, the load of wood that was stacked on the cart. The book tucked under Yaakov's arm was a slim volume of Alexander Pushkin's poems. How she wished she could accept the book, since all of hers had burned in the fire.

"Let me talk to my grandfather," he said. "I'm sure we can work something out until you get on your feet again." As he bent down to ease the bundle off his shoulder, he dropped a sheaf of papers, which Leah helped pick up.

The papers were flyers announcing a meeting being held for all interested workers in the province. Alarmed, she whispered, "This is dangerous to carry around. Be careful."

"Please, I am just alerting people. We do nothing wrong." But he also kept his voice low. "Perhaps you would like to come and see. We are just a group of Jews who want things to be better."

She pulled him inside the cellar door. "Are you crazy? I've heard how they kill workers who protest or hold meetings." She was about to tell him to go on his way, but something stopped her. Wasn't she tired of things being bad for the poor with trouble especially for the Jews if they spoke out? Didn't she want things to be better instead of having to grovel to Vaselik asking for her job back? Why not at least hear what these people have to say. "I'd have to bring the children; I can't leave them here alone."

"Of course," Yaakov said. "You'll ride with me. It's being held in the next village, less than ten miles. I'll come back at sundown. Dress warmly. In the meantime, keep the things I brought, you need them."

***

It was chilly riding in the dark, but the two children were bundled under thick, wooly blankets that Yaakov provided. Leah brought a jar of tea and some dried apples as a snack. The moon played tag with the clouds, illuminating the countryside, making it seem almost a festive occasion. Leah noticed that Yaakov was older than her first impression, he had the beginnings of lines around his eyes, which were a soft grey-blue, in contrast to his young face.

His youthful enthusiasm had made him a bit reckless in inviting her to this meeting, not knowing what her sentiments were. Of course, she'd never betray him, but he didn't really know her and even a whisper of these meetings in the wrong ear could be a one-way ticket to jail or worse, courtesy of the government. She began to feel a bit uneasy, perhaps she had been too impetuous in accompanying him, but taking a chance also renewed her sense of adventure for the first time since she was a young girl. And the possibility that she would meet people who wanted to make a difference in the world finally won out over her fears.

She wished the ride was in daylight, so she could see the countryside. Getting out of Koritz was an adventure itself, but at night she could only make out the dim shapes of tall, dark evergreen trees, moonlight sparkling on their top-most branches. After two hours, they stopped at a small house, which was set back from the road, out of the sight of any inquisitive passerby. A field behind the house stretched out to the woods. The windows of the house were covered by heavy curtains allowing no sign of life in the house to seep through, reminding her of her first visit to Freydel's house.

Yaakov tethered the horse to one of the trees next to the other wagons and horses, and left a bag of oats for Drushka to eat. Inside, Leah tucked the boys into the corner of a small room, where several other children were already asleep. They looked like rag dolls all tumbled together. Benny immediately stretched out on a cushion and Joseph leaned against him. Despite bouncing over rutted roads, both children had managed to nap during the long ride, but in the warmth of the room they had no problem falling asleep again. Only children, Leah thought, could adapt so quickly, totally ignoring the loud voices coming from the next room.

She followed Yaakov and sat down close to him, observing how young many of the people were, late teens and early twenties, with only a few in their thirties. The man at the front of the room who appeared to be a leader, was older, perhaps in his forties. The place had been cleared of all furniture, but was crowded with people standing about, sitting on cushions or leaning up against the wall.

Leah overheard snatches of conversations that seemed to be diametrically opposed to each other. Some people insisted on immediate reform from the government, ready to storm the Czar's palace again, angry at the government's slow pace or lack of pace, while others talked of being more cautious, not wanting to upset the authorities, more worried about the consequences.

One man stood up haltingly sharing his experience of Bloody Sunday. "Once the soldiers started shooting, everyone ran, some fell and got caught under the feet of the others. There was screaming, no one expected this. I had left my village without permission. If I had been stopped by the police I would have been arrested." Then he straightened up and declared, "I'd do it again."

A woman, who had recently experienced an attack on her village, argued the other side, that Jews should keep themselves separate from Russian culture as the only way to preserve Jewish traditions.

"Russia has always tried to convert us or kill us. They used to kidnap our boys and conscript them for twenty-five years in the army hoping they would give up their religion. Now they restrict most of us from working in any profitable jobs and force us to live in an area away from the cities." She was immediately shouted down by a young man.

"That's the old way," the young man said, jumping up from his corner on the floor. "We should push for the chance to be educated and join in the main society. Then we will have a better opportunity to be accepted and become successful."

The woman, called Masha, argued back. "Money is not the only thing. That's what the gentiles always accuse us of," she said contemptuously. "Many have been killed merely because they were Jews. It's up to us to work to preserve our traditions."

The room grew quiet for a moment, then the leader, Josef, reminded everyone that quarreling with each other doesn't help the cause even if it was the Jewish way, which made everyone laugh and lightened the mood. Before the meeting broke up, a young girl named Sarah asked to read a poem written by Vera Figner, one of the movement's heroines. The last lines went:

And our long, drawn-out suffering shall

Call to the younger generation

To fight for liberty.

Leah had never thought about ordinary citizens changing the way a country treated its people, certainly not Jews. They had always been treated as outsiders, although Jews had lived in Russia for generations. Even her father, learned in both religious and secular matters, never thought to raise his voice in protest or believe that his voice could be heard by Moscow. How extraordinary that these young people risked so much to meet and plan protests. And so many tonight were women. The Bund, Yaakov explained, was started to help workers and from the beginning had the involvement of many women. It was exciting to hear how they worked and fought right alongside of their male colleagues. In a different situation, Leah would have chosen the side of the marchers.

Yaakov definitely sided with the hotheads. He was ready to storm the Czar's palace, if that's what it would take to force change. Even the prospect of another Bloody Sunday, where hundreds of protesters had been shot, did not deter him. She was impressed by the passion of his beliefs. The people she had known had always been so cautious.

The ride home was quiet, except for the steady clip-clop of Drushka's slow pace, a silver sliver of moon lighting the way. Leah finally broke the silence, asking, "Isn't there a big risk that the authorities will find out about your meetings?" The possibility of reprisals still worried her.

Yaakov held the reins loosely, letting Drushka go his own pace

"When my grandfather was young, he was sickly," he said. "His lungs were very weak. His mother was afraid that the authorities or one of those people who got hired to kidnap children for the army, would take him away and he'd never survive his conscription. So she dressed him in skirts, covered his head with a shawl and kept him in the background whenever strangers came around, so he would pass as a female. To this day he feels guilty that he didn't stand up and fight the government instead of hiding in women's clothes. I fight not only for myself, but also for my grandfather."

It was so late when they reached Koritz, Leah suggested that Yaakov sleep in Sophia's barn.

"It's too dangerous to ride home," she said, worried about bandits or rogue members of the Black Hundreds. He took blankets from the wagon and she promised him breakfast before he left in the morning.

"Thank you for coming tonight," he said, spreading his blankets over a pile of hay. He regarded her so intently that Leah blushed.

Looking around he said, "You know this barn could be turned into a new home for you. It would be easy to put up a couple of walls and a new door."

"It belonged to my neighbor who died," she reminded him. "I don't feel right taking it." Sometimes she thought that Sophia's spirit still hovered there, not so ready to let go as she had seemed the night she died. "Besides I have no money to pay you and your grandfather."

"Zayda likes you and would want to help. Think about it."

Early in the next morning, Leah discovered that Yaakov had already left before she awoke. She remembered his offer and hoped he was serious about helping her rebuild.

A short while later, she heard the rumbling of a cart and thought Yaakov had forgotten something and come back. Instead it was Sasha bringing a large package of food, including a live chicken, some potatoes, dried apples, a bag of meal, tea, sugar and candies for Benny.

"How are you young master?" Sasha asked, patting Benny's head. But the orderly hesitated when Leah questioned him about the gift.

"Sasha, you'll get into trouble doing this," she said, marveling at his generosity. "Your captain won't like it. I'm afraid for you." This food would keep them eating for well over a week.

"Not to worry Missus," he said, looking around the cramped cellar, squinting in the dim light.

"But I've seen his temper," she said. "I know he's capable of beating you."

"That's just the way of army officers, you mustn't mind," he replied. Under her insistent questioning, he finally admitted, "It's the Captain who sent this food."

"You're just saying that so I won't worry." She looked at him, his eyes like small dark buttons, but he turned very red.

"No, ma'am," he insisted. "You're right. I couldn't take all this food from the pantry without his permission. I think he feels bad about letting you go, but he can never admit it."

"Are you really telling the truth, Sasha?" It seemed improbable that Vaselik was so unpredictable and yet show such kindness.

***

Vaselik sat at his desk looking over reports without any enthusiasm or effort to absorb what they said. He'd received new orders to be on the alert for underground groups which might be planning protests or other revolutionary activities. He felt mired in the sludge of political affairs when all he longed for was a battle where the lines were clearly drawn; you knew who your enemy was, you were armed and ready for the kill. If he had a choice, he would gladly give up this military charade. But what else was he fit for? The family estates had been lost in a swirl of debts after his father's suicide. His beautiful mother returned to her family and sent him off to military school, grudgingly paid for by his grandfather. Weighed down with sorrow, she had begun a downward spiral into a never-ending depression which finally claimed her life two years later. During that time she never allowed him to come to Moscow or ever visited him. He believed it was because she did not want him to see her in that sick, degraded condition. After she died, his grandfather cut off all contact, too upset by the sight of the grandson, who so closely resembled the man he blamed for his daughter's death.

"Sasha," Vaselik yelled. When no one answered, Vaselik remembered that he had sent him to take food to the Peretz woman. He hadn't been able to shake off his guilt over her accusations, her grief over those combs. He hoped that sending food would assuage his unease over Leah's outburst.

Certainly his men were happier that she no longer worked at the camp. All they were interested in was their own petty pilfering. Vaselik, like many of his counterparts, was on constant alert about grumbling in the ranks which could escalate into real trouble. There had been more accounts of mutinous soldiers from elsewhere in the country. It was just as well that he not add to his problems by keeping Leah as the camp cook.

He poured a shot of vodka into his mug of tea. Almost unnoticed at first, his drinking now began earlier and earlier in the day. If he thought about it, he could trace it all back to the evening when his three army friends came to visit. Now some mornings he even began breakfast with a quick swig of vodka.

Sometimes when he drank he could hear his grandfather's condemnation the last time they met. "Your father was a wastrel and a drunkard. Take care that you don't end up like him. He not only killed himself, he killed my daughter, too!"

The old bastard acted as if he was the only one who had suffered. Vaselik had lost both parents and now had no further funds to help support him. Not a smile nor an encouraging word ever came from that miserable skinflint. Once when his grandmother took pity on him and secretly gave him a little money, his grandfather found out and made him return it, treating him like a thief instead of a grandson. But more than anyone, Vaselik laid all his troubles at the feet of that damned Jewish overseer.

Sasha stood at the door, giving a slight cough. "Captain, Missus Peretz is here. She'd like a word with you."

"What? Why? Oh alright, send her in." Vaselik would not allow another hysterical scene. He stood as she entered.

"Captain," she said. "I just wanted to thank you for your generosity. My children and I appreciate it very much." Leah was embarrassed to show her gratitude, it was easier to speak if she did not look directly at him.

"Sasha is a fool. That was to be kept completely quiet. It's nothing."

"I'd like to offer to cook you a dinner to show my appreciation," she said. "No charge of course," she added. "Unless you think the Widow Popov will mind." Leah could not suppress a small smile, knowing how irritated that woman would be if Leah returned to her kitchen.

Her whole face lights up when she smiles, Vaselik thought. She's almost beautiful. "I accept," he said. "Let's do it tomorrow. And of course I'll provide the food."

It had to be just gratitude that motivated her offer to cook dinner. But when Leah entered the office and saw Vaselik standing there, her heart took an extra beat, like any foolish adolescent girl. She couldn't deny that he was handsome, despite that scowl on his face. Still he was her enemy, even if he had been kind to her and the children. Perhaps too kind. She should be wary of such generosity, but today she saw his eyes soften when she offered to cook for him. She noted that he stood when she came into the office, like any gentleman would do for a lady. This all left her too confused at a time when she needed to have her wits about her and stay very much in control.

chapter 11

LEAH STOPPED COOKING long enough to nurse Joseph, annoyed that the Widow Popov watched her through a crack in the open kitchen door. Let the old witch stand guard if she wants, Leah thought, there's nothing here I'd stoop to steal. But she did envy that the widow had this refuge of a kitchen and a house which stood unharmed. And still the woman constantly complained.

In Leah's opinion, if anyone had the right to complain it was her. Once, she lived in a house like this one near the Pripyat River, in sight of apple orchards, safe with her father and brothers. During her marriage to Morris, as poor as they were, there was always a roof over their heads. Everything changed that fateful night. Covetousness might be a sin, but Leah couldn't help wish that it was in her power to take this place away from that woman.

Looking down at Joseph sucking happily, her mood softened. His dark eyes looked back at her, a happier version of Morris's face. The baby's complacent nature reminded Leah of him. Like Morris, Joseph rarely complained. He reached up to curl a strand of her hair around his fingers, playing with it as if it were his new favorite toy. When she smiled down at him, he returned it with an extra giggle. As long as her children were healthy, she was truly blessed.

When he was full and content, she put Joseph back on the blanket near the warm stove and gave him the rag doll that Yaakov had brought him. Soon his soft, regular breathing told her he was asleep, while his big brother built a fort with snow and mud outside the kitchen door.

As promised, Sasha brought in the food: a fat duckling, yams the size of small melons, dried beans, rice, a jar of plum preserves to slather on a freshly baked sponge cake. The Widow never stopped watching Leah during the preparations, looking disappointed that she had nothing to complain about to Vaselik. Leah also guessed that the Widow was upset when Vaselik announced that he planned to dine alone and didn't invite her to eat with him, although he left instructions for Leah to leave a full plate of food for the Widow.

In addition to the bedroom that Vaselik rented, he had access to the dining room whenever he wished, the room where he had entertained his army friends. But this evening he decided to use the sitting area next to his room. It was smaller and cozier than the formal dining room, with its heavy, musty drapes that covered windows that were rarely opened. He had used the larger room to impress his comrades, with its carved mahogany table, high-backed chairs and sideboard, but tonight he preferred comfort, lounging at the low table, on cushions, next to the fireplace, like some Arab potentate.

The smaller room, which had been the Widow's dressing area in happier times, was decorated with a lighter touch, cream-colored walls, a rose tapestry chaise and a mother-of-pearl inlaid writing table, which tonight served as the dining table. Leah found it hard to imagine the frowsy widow in such a delicate environment and it also surprised her that the strict military captain chose to dine in such feminine surroundings.

Leah served dinner on a large silver tray that she discovered in the cupboard, the silver etched in scenes of centaurs chasing buxom maidens, the handles entwined grape vines. It was probably one of the last vestiges of the widow's more prosperous life before her husband died. Leah tried to be more sympathetic about the widow's misfortune, but instead her heart hardened, feeling little remorse for gloating over the widow's bad fortune. Morris would never have approved of Leah's attitude, reminding her that God forbade rejoicing over the downfall of your enemies. Even now she knew no matter how hard she might try, she could never live up to Morris's Torah.

Vaselik ate slowly, savoring the leisurely pace to the meal. He poured some wine as Leah brought in cake and tea.

"This dinner was superb," he said, mopping up the last of the gravy with a piece of bread. He leaned over to the fireplace and lit his cigar with a taper. "Where did you learn to cook?"

"At home, Captain. I was the only girl and my mother was often very sick." She had been a vain teenager, proud of how well she ran the household, taking good care of her father and brothers, sometimes ashamed that she enjoyed being in charge since it came as the result of her mother being so ill.

"Ahh," he said. "We have that in common." He poured more wine, motioning for her to sit. "My mother, too, became very ill after my father died."

Having polite conversation with Vaselik seemed strange, as if they were friends chatting over a meal. "Please, sir, I don't wish to intrude on your dinner."

He poured a second glass, indicating that it was for her, but she shook her head, becoming even more uncomfortable. "Then join me for some tea and cake, please," he said.

"No thank you, but if I could have a piece for my boy, he'd be thrilled." She remembered how giddy she had felt in his presence yesterday and was unsure of how she should act with him.

"Woman, I'm not a monster, you know. Of course, your boy can have some cake. He can have the whole damned thing. Now sit down, please, for a moment." He moved the tray of cake and tea to the floor and directed her to sit on the ottoman.

She perched on the edge, nervously like a bird about to take flight. "My children are alone in the kitchen, Captain."

"You are just a few steps away from the kitchen. Surely no harm can come to them." He studied her, noting her apparent nervousness. "Do I make you so uncomfortable?" he asked.

"Truthfully, yes," she said. "In my community married women don't spend time alone with men not their husbands."

"Are you afraid?" he asked, moving his chair directly in front of her.

"Should I be?" she answered, getting her courage back. She stood, about to dart away, but Vaselik stopped her, took her hands and studied them intently.

"These hands shouldn't have to work so hard. They should belong to a lady of leisure, one more adapted to pleasure."

Leah was acutely aware of how red and chapped her hands had become. She wasn't sure if he was mocking her. He started to raise her hands to his lips, but Leah pulled away. Suddenly there was a baby's cry from the kitchen and Benny called for her.

"Let me pass, please," she said. She ran to Joseph, who had awakened in a sweat, needing to be changed into dry clothes. His face felt warm, but she assumed it was from being so close to the stove.

She said to herself that her nervousness was because of the children. Still the moment Vaselik held her hands she was afraid. No one had ever looked at her as he did, coolly appraising her, offering compliments. No one she knew had ever talked about the pursuit of pleasure, as if it were something to which she might be entitled. Even the most affluent Jews did not think of pleasure as a right. Only in her novels did characters pursue pleasure, but invariably in those stories, they paid the price with tragic outcomes. Enjoying Vaselik's attention excited Leah. It was a new, strange sensation, a physical pleasure that flooded her body.

She picked up Joseph, who hungrily reached out to be nursed. Then she saw Vaselik standing at the open kitchen door, watching her. Mortified, she turned away, shielding herself and the baby from his glance and after a moment he walked away.

Leah didn't let Joseph continue to nurse, immediately wrapping him, gathering her things, and hurrying Benny out the door. She strode so fast that Benny had difficulty in keeping up. He called out, "Mama, please wait. What's the matter?"

"I'm sorry," she said. "It's very cold. I want to get you home as fast as possible."

She took his hand in hers, feeling the small bones of his fingers, but remembering Vaselik's strong grip clasping her hand. She held the boy so tightly he winced. If she hadn't run away, what might have happened?

Nothing, she insisted to herself, but nagging doubts arose. It was dangerous to be around Vaselik. There had to be a way to earn money without begging him for her job back. There was enough food to last awhile, but she had to find an income and a better place to live than the cellar. She thought again of Yaakov's offer to fix up Sophia's barn. Leah wasn't superstitious, so why fret about the spirit of a dead woman who could do her no harm.

chapter 12

THE FREQUENT VISITS to Leah's door for help with the sick started with Avram Lichtenstein asking about his young daughter, who was congested and coughing. Then Rifka Solomon came late one night, worried about her baby son, who was at home burning with fever. Mr. Holstein remembered that Leah had medicinal herbs and requested help for his elderly mother, who felt too weak to get out of bed.

Leah feared that the illnesses came from the dead who had lain unburied too long. Villagers looked to Leah to heal them with the cures and remedies in Anna's satchel. They chose Leah who lived close by instead of taking the long walk to Freydel's house. After only a few days of non stop requests, Leah felt besieged and began turning people away, urging them to go to Freydel. When Rifka's baby died, people stopped coming, realizing that some problems were too great for Leah.

Her nights remained filled with bad dreams. Sometimes she was lost on a strange, dark road, tormented by voices crying out for help. On a night she dreamt about her family, she was awakened by Benny shaking her as hard as he could. Opening her eyes, she heard the labored sound of Joseph coughing.

"Mama, wake up," Benny said, pulling at her shoulder to get up. "Something's wrong with Joseph."

Leah touched the baby. His skin was hot and sweaty; he was gasping and coughing at the same time. She picked him up, expecting him to calm down but his body jerked with each gasp. Then for a moment, he seemed to quiet, but when she tried to nurse him he stiffened and turned away from her full breast.

"It's just a cold," she said to reassure Benny. But the baby felt feverish, just like some of the other children who had come for help. He began coughing again, each cough ending in a whoop like a bird in distress. Leah was terrified. If he had the whooping sickness, how could she heal him? And what if Benny got sick too?

"Benny, dress warmly and take your blanket right now and go to Sophia's barn. I want you to stay there until I tell you it's alright to come back. You can't be near the baby right now."

Benny looked stricken. "But Mama, I could just stay in the corner out of the way."

"No," she insisted, "you mustn't get sick. Take your things and I'll bring you some breakfast in a little while. Please, Benny, do as I say."

Leah brewed tea with elder and yarrow, adding a little peppermint and hyssop to ease the congestion. She was thankful to Anna and Freydel for their collection of herbs, relieved that she had saved some for her own children. Despite her misgivings, she offered a quick prayer to God, even if He was her divine nemesis. Maybe today He'd take time to listen.

"You and I don't get along," she muttered fiercely. "But Joseph's just a baby, too young to be of any use to You. Help him, please." Morris's praying had always irritated her, because it encouraged his inaction, but when it came to her children, she would take no chances. She just hoped God wouldn't think of her as too hypocritical.

She gave Benny a quick hug, and pushed him out the door, just as Yaakov pulled up to her door in his wagon.

Before he could jump down, Leah ran to him, pleading, "Yaakov, please I need your help. It's the baby." She implored him to go to Freydel's house and bring the old woman back to help Joseph. "Tell her I think it's the whooping sickness. His bouts of coughing frighten me. So many people are sick here in Koritz. She must come."

"Don't worry, Leah. I'll drag her here if necessary."

She tried feeding drops of tea to Joseph, but he couldn't catch his breath long enough to swallow. She used steam from a pot of boiling water to ease his breathing. The coughing sometimes stopped for a moment, only to begin again until she panicked wondering how much more his little body could take.

She held him, softly crooning a Yiddish lullaby that her mother had sung to Leah and her brothers, one that Leah had sung to baby Rachel. She kissed his cheek, and sang, *"Schluff, tireah kind, schluff sisa klein faiglah. Sleep dear child, sleep sweet little bird."*

There was a knock on the cellar door, and Gittel peered in. "I saw Benny crying outside. What's wrong?"

The women hadn't spoken since Gittel heard that Leah was working for Vaselik, and they didn't reconcile even after Leah left the job. Still Leah needed her neighbor's help now.

"I'm afraid that the baby might have the coughing sickness," Leah said. "He can hardly catch his breath and he makes that awful sound, like a dying bird."

"What can I do?" Gittel tried not to show her alarm at the baby's coughing, his non-stop crying.

"Help me with Benny, please. If you could take him some breakfast this morning, I would be very grateful." The baby began coughing again, clenching his eyes tight, his body stiff.

"I've sent for Freydel," Leah said. All those babies she had lost, even Anna Vashenko with all her skills had not been able to save them. But Joseph could not die.

Gittel left, promising to feed Benny. The minutes dragged slowly, and Leah thought she might go crazy waiting. Finally, Freydel and Yaakov arrived, but the old woman's face was anything but encouraging as she listened to the whooping sound that Joseph was making.

"I'm going to cup him to draw out the fever," Freydel said. She took three small glass cups from her bag, warming them over the pot of steaming water. She tested them on her wrist then placed them on Joseph's back while Leah tried to hold the baby still. But he squirmed and cried, making him cough even more.

"No, take them off," Leah begged. "It's making it worse." Small dark circles remained on his back after Freydel removed the cups.

"The only thing left to do now is to keep him warm, give him small sips of hyssop tea, but no peppermint, it's too irritating. And keep him upright so he can breathe better." Freydel's grim expression further frightened Leah. "You must just wait and see," the old woman said, motioning to Yaakov that she was ready to leave.

"Oh God, please don't go," Leah implored.

"There's nothing more I can do here. The illness has to run its own course."

Freydel took her bag and went out the door. Outside, other villagers recognized her and begged her to look at their sick children. Reluctantly she followed one of the women, leaving Yaakov to wait with the horse.

When Gittel returned to let Leah know that Benny was warm and well-fed in the barn, Leah asked her to take Benny's prayer books, so he could study and keep distracted from worrying about Joseph.

Joseph lay against Leah's shoulder, quiet for a moment, his mouth making little sucking noises. Who was this little being, so sweet and un-complaining? The baby adapted more easily to circumstances than even Benny, who had become so fearful since the night of the attack. This child had done nothing to deserve this suffering. How could she believe in a God that had so little compassion for small children and babies or good men like Morris, who willingly put their faith in the unknown and unseen?

A loud knock at the door startled her and Sasha marched in with a large parcel of food. At the sight of his good-natured, little elfin face, Leah burst into tears. That seemed to propel Joseph into a deep, hacking coughing spell. The orderly looked dismayed, totally unsure as to what he should do. Stammering, he asked, "Missus, what is it?"

"The baby is very sick," Leah said. "Even Freydel, the village healer said she can do nothing. I'm so afraid."

"I'll go back to camp. The Captain may know the whereabouts of a nearby doctor." He ran out before she could utter a word.

Less than an hour later, Sasha returned, followed by a young man in uniform, about thirty, surprised at being brought to this cellar with only a woman and child, instead of the military emergency he was prepared to answer. Sasha introduced him as Dr. Peter Morozov.

Leah saw him checking the damp cellar walls, the fire burning near the entrance, the pallets of straw-filled blankets on the dirt floor. His manner softened, saying, "The Captain's orderly said it was urgent." Wiping the dust from his hands, Dr. Morozov took out his stethoscope and listened to the baby's chest. When the cold metal touched him, Joseph broke into a bad bout of coughing, ending with the bird-like whooping.

That sound continued to panic Leah. "Doctor, help him please. Is he going to die?"

Morozov looked at the baby's eyes, ears and throat, while Joseph squirmed and coughed, twisted and wriggled in the doctor's hands. Morozov muttered to Sasha, "Give me a battlefield injury and I'm your man. But with babies, it's much harder." His tone with Leah remained quiet, soothing, "Mother, I'll leave you this narcotic to use as a last resort, if he can't stop coughing. Just a drop or two. For now just keep him warm and continue with the tea."

The doctor had no more to offer than Freydel. Winds began to kick up outside, whistling like some alien spirit. She worried that the sound might frighten Benny, so she asked Sasha if he could go and comfort Benny. She had never thought of herself as superstitious, but now everything appeared to her like a sign, a portent of things to come. The sound of the wind was a bad omen, but the new moon tonight might be a good one. Perhaps it meant that Morris was looking down, protecting his youngest son. But Joseph continued to cough and wouldn't take the tea, so she decided that maybe she was the bad omen for the child. Was she being punished for working for Vaselik, for accepting his help, and worst of all, for enjoying his attentions? And all those complaints that Morris had endured during her marriage. Perhaps there was a God and He was going to punish her again by taking away her baby.

Suddenly there was a new bout of coughing, so severe it seemed to shake the breath out of Joseph. His face began to turn bluish, his eyes became glazed. She wept, holding him against her heart, desperate to transfer her life into him.

Like a ghostly apparition, Vaselik appeared at the door. He saw the baby's extreme distress and very firmly said, "Let me see the child. Perhaps I can help." Leah shook her head, terrified of letting go of the baby. "Please, let me see him," Vaselik insisted, "just for a moment."

Talking softly, Vaselik forced Leah's fingers open, until he was able to take the baby from her. Sitting down, he laid the baby across his lap and began to breathe directly into Joseph's mouth, continuing in regular intervals, until the child's chest finally began to move more normally, and color returned to Joseph's face.

Leah overwhelmed with relief, grabbed Vaselik's hand, kissing it in gratitude. She took the baby, stroked his cheek, saw his normal color return, heard that his breathing was easier and even.

"Thank you, you saved him. How did you know what to do?" she asked. She was embarrassed by her spontaneous moment of gratitude, not wanting him to misunderstand.

"It's a method I saw used on the battlefield." He stood up, ready to leave. "Sasha told me that the doctor did not offer you much so I came to see if I could be of any help. I'm glad I was here."

"You've been more than good to us, but it baffles me since I know how badly you regard Jews."

"There are good reasons for my enmity, but I told you before, I'm no monster. A child suffers, isn't that enough?" He looked discomfited by his admission.

"There is no greater sorrow than losing a child," Leah said, looking down at Joseph. "Even the ones who barely live to see the light of day, stay with you forever and you always mourn them."

She had never talked about her losses before. It was strange that she should discuss her feelings with this man. But he had practically willed Joseph back to life, something she was unable to do. And, she could not forget the touch of his hand. Her face grew warm and she turned away so he couldn't see her.

"You never seemed to be afraid of me," he said, "yet you're always running away or like now, hiding your face. Why is that?"

"I told you, I'm not used to talking alone with a man who is not my husband. In the eyes of the community, I'm still a married woman." This was partly true, although these were the very conventions that she tried to rebel against all her life. She certainly couldn't admit how extraordinary he made her feel, instead she was talking like any one of the small-minded villagers.

Vaselik barely admitted his own feelings. True, she was attractive, even dressed as she was, with those dark eyes set against almost luminous skin, but still she was not a great beauty. He had wooed and flirted with far more beautiful, elegant women. She was not as seductive as the always available camp followers who clustered around military barracks. But his affairs always left him unsatisfied, like having a meal of sweets with no sustenance. This woman intrigued him, her spirit, her courage, her unflinching dignity in times of calamity.

But, what could he want with her? As a Russian officer, it was dangerous to enter into any liaison with a Jew—it could anger his superiors and enrage the entire village towards both of them. Even if she agreed. Still, he never backed down in a challenge, not if he decided that it was something he wanted.

chapter 13

THE BABY SLOWLY recuperated. He remained fussy, restless, frequently not interested in nursing, other times ravenous until Leah's breasts ached. It was absolutely essential in order to protect the children from further illness that she secure a warm home as soon as possible. Benny returned to the cellar resentful, as if their plight was somehow her fault. He acted angry and irritable towards her, but she tried to understand how hard life had become for him, especially without his father. Morris might have had deficiencies as a husband, but his son worshiped him. She had no one to help shoulder her problems. She felt so utterly alone.

Yaakov returned to see how Joseph was progressing and brought a cart filled with materials to turn the barn into a livable space. "That was why I came the other day," he said. "I thought about all of you living in this damp cellar. So I spoke to my grandfather, who also insists that you accept our help."

"I promise," Leah said, "that no matter how long it takes, I'll repay you both." She brought out the pair of silver combs and offered them as partial payment, but he refused to accept them. "My grandfather and I can wait until you get more settled," he said.

That afternoon she went to see Haim Holstein, to get his permission to use Sophia's barn. Holstein, as the town's most prominent businessman was also the town leader and Leah wanted him to give his blessing. She didn't feel comfortable just taking it without an official okay. Holstein's face was like a map of all the recent events, lines deeply etched across his face, his hair and beard totally gray. He grew pensive describing the problems Koritz faced in trying to restore itself to pre-pogrom days.

"Our benevolent society is stretched to the breaking point," he said. "Everybody needs help and we've pleaded for funds from other communities, including those in other countries, but it's taking so long.

"However, since there are no Wolf family members left to claim the barn, and you and your children are in dire need of immediate warm shelter, you have permission to make it into a proper living space. But in return, you must promise to do future mitzvahs for others who are in need."

So with Holstein's consent, Leah and Yaakov started unloading the cart, piled with wood, tools, pots, pans, blankets, an old iron bedstead and a large cradle for the baby. She was overwhelmed by Yaakov and his grandfather's generosity. Even though she knew that the old man was fond of her, she wondered if Yaakov was really behind all this help. He was becoming like another brother to her.

In the past, the village's Jewish Benevolent Society helped feed the homeless, especially on Shabbos and holidays, collected clothing, provided burial rituals or gave a bridal dowry to a needy girl. Now short of funds, the Society sent two teenaged boys to assist Yaakov with the work on the barn.

It was really only a large shed, but it had housed a cow and a few chickens and there was a hayloft, accessible by ladder. They erected an interior wall to divide the space into a kitchen and bedroom, cut a window to let in some light, added a proper door and put down wooden boards as a floor to keep out the damp. The hayloft space was left as an additional sleeping area, so in the future Leah could take in a boarder to earn extra money. Not that anyone had much money now, but if she couldn't get cash, she might barter services with someone.

Leah realized that if circumstances continued to be desperate, she would have to consider selling that cup and spice box, still buried since the night of the pogrom. Along with the combs, they were not only family mementos but the only valuable things she had left. She'd sell them if absolutely necessary, but for now they stayed safely underground.

The prospect of a new, improved place cheered Benny, who wanted to help, but generally made a nuisance of himself, getting underfoot, running back and forth exclaiming, "Mama, look at the nail I just hammered," until the inevitable happened and he banged his finger instead of the nail. He immediately reverted back to babyhood, running to his mother to kiss away the pain.

After more than two days of working from early morning until past dark it was suddenly finished. They finished just before Shabbos and to celebrate the first Sabbath in the newly renovated home, Leah cooked a big pot of soup brimming with the last of her chicken, onions and carrots. She used the new hearth, although Yaakov promised to look for a small, old stove on his next trip. The rescued samovar, abandoned and blackened during the attack, now sat freshly shined in an honored spot, brewing tea. She invited the two young boys to join Yaakov, the children and her for Shabbos supper. They all sat on blankets on the floor using an old shaky table that Leah had found. She lit the candles, reciting the blessing over them. Yaakov said the blessings for the bread and the little sip of wine they each had, a present from Mr. Holstein.

Benny blessed the memory of his father. "Papa, we miss you," he said. "Don't forget us now that you're up in heaven with the angels."

"I'm sure he's watching over us, Benny," Leah said, her fingers lightly touching his cheek. Sometimes she actually did think she felt a whisper of breath on her face, even stronger whenever she considered doing something that Morris would not have approved.

Leah toasted Yaakov with a special thank you for turning the shed into a real home. The fireplace would help keep them warm, even though every so often the chimney did not draw properly and they had to open the door to air out the room of smoke. That night Yaakov slept in the loft space, but awoke early, ready to return home, even though it meant travelling on the Sabbath.

"I don't like leaving my grandfather alone for too long," he told Leah. "The neighbors are kind, but he's so frail now, I worry." He jumped up on the wagon and said quietly, "I'll be back with the stove and perhaps you'll go to another meeting with me."

She nodded, but it worried her that he spoke so easily about his plans outside where anyone could overhear him. Surely he knew that anyone suspected of rebellion or reform could be arrested. And then as if to confirm her worst fears, she saw Vaselik, on horseback, riding towards her as Yaakov drove away.

"Good morning, Widow Peretz."

Leah hated being called "Widow Peretz," as if she were in the same category as that irritating Widow Popov. At the same time she couldn't help noticing how well he sat his horse, tall and straight, like a warrior about to go into battle. His expression was again non-committal; gone was the look of compassion he had begun to show her. Yet she couldn't deny that his mere presence excited her, which both frightened and thrilled her.

"It seems you've already started to take in boarders," Vaselik said, pointing at Yaakov, disappearing down the road.

"Peddler Foreman's grandson was kind enough to help rebuild the barn, along with some boys from the village. Thanks to them and to your kindness, my children have been able to survive."

"Really? How noble of him. Perhaps you will offer me some tea. I'd like to see this miracle of house-building that has been accomplished so quickly." Vaselik dismounted and entered before she had a chance to agree or protest.

At the door he stopped, seeing Benny in the corner with his prayer book, next to Joseph, asleep near the hearth. "Here boy, catch," he said, taking a dark red apple from the coat slung around his shoulders and tossed it to Benny, who happily caught it.

The boy looked at Leah for permission, and when she nodded, he immediately bit into it, then stopped red-faced. "Would you like some Mama?" he asked.

"No Benny. It's all for you."

"Go outside," Vaselik instructed the boy, "and give my horse some water, and make sure he's tied securely." Looking around, he smiled, but without warmth. "So with this palace, I suppose you'll no longer be in need of any more help from Sasha or me." He walked around the small room, his boots sounding like claps of thunder on the bare wooden floorboards.

Leah poured some tea into a glass, brought out a cube of her precious sugar and waited quietly as Vaselik checked everything as if he were on a military inspection. There were no chairs so he stood before her holding the glass of steaming tea, staring intently at her.

"I'll give you Jews credit," he said. "You are all resilient. Nothing seems to keep you down for long."

"Are you disappointed, Captain?" She was confused by his arrogance. "You usually blame us for everything." No matter how the conversation started they always seem to be at odds. A little like her days with Morris.

"And now some of you are busy fomenting trouble." He sipped his tea, but watched Leah closely for her reaction. "Are you sure that the peddler isn't one of those renegades?"

"Excuse me, Captain, but I told you who he was and what he was doing here. Is there some further problem?"

For a long moment of silence, he continued staring at her, then he put down his glass and pulled her close, whispering, "You're my problem. It would be better for me if you weren't." Then unexpectedly, he kissed her, long and hard.

The pressure of his mouth, his arms holding her, his breath warm on her skin, all made her lightheaded. Pull away now before it's too late, she thought. This is all madness, but she returned his kiss. Then like a patient slowly regaining her sanity, she broke apart, putting the table between them.

"You must leave," she said, upset by the kiss and the pleasure it gave her.

"It makes no sense to me either, but I am drawn to you," he whispered. "And now I know you feel the same."

"I'm grateful to you, that is all. I can have no other feelings for you." Her eyes began to fill, but she would not let herself cry and look weak.

Benny came in, upset by Leah's expression. "Mama, are you alright?" He ran to her, glaring at Vaselik. "Did he hurt you?" Benny ran straight at Vaselik swinging at him wildly.

"Easy, boy," Vaselik said, deflecting the boy's fist. "Your mother is upset about other things."

Vaselik left, riding off angry for admitting his emotions and being rebuffed like some bumbling adolescent. He would get over this humiliation even though he was not used to being refused. Then he thought, no matter what she said, she **had** responded, despite all her protestations. He wheeled Nicademus around and galloped back to the house. He jumped down and barged inside, ignoring Leah's stunned expression and Benny's angry dash towards him.

"You do care," he shouted at Leah. "Don't try to deny it." Then he strode out, not waiting for any response.

Leah stood there, her heart pounding, her head bursting. Who was she more afraid of, herself or Vaselik?

Benny ran scared to her, wrapping himself around her knees. "It's alright," Leah said. "The captain didn't mean to scare you. That's just how soldiers are sometimes. Go fix up your corner of the bedroom."

The boy relaxed and went inside to put his things on a small shelf in the corner above his cot. Yaakov had made the cot out of strong material stretched and nailed between two long pieces of wood, attached to four short legs to raise the cot off the ground. Benny arranged the soldiers that Sasha had given him on the shelf, next to the red-stained prayer book that had belonged to his father.

Leah stayed in the kitchen, drinking tea, trying to calm her mind.

chapter 14

LEAH BUSIED HERSELF hoping she would stop thinking about Vaselik. Usually the daily struggle of existence completely exhausted her: looking for food, keeping the new place clean, lugging water in from the well, cooking, searching for firewood, taking care of the children, but she returned again and again to him. She'd picture how tall he was, remember how his thick hair gleamed, how like some healing angel he had swooped in to save Joseph. But most especially, she returned to the moment of their kiss.

She was alarmed that it meant so much to her. Growing up, her brothers had teased her because she had been such a romantic, emotional at the change in the seasons, affected by flowers, melancholy over the sound of the wind blowing through the trees, breathless at seeing the night sky filled with stars. Her romantic notions were shaped by the books she read, which to her brothers' horror, were mainly novels. When her mother became ill, she locked away her ideas and dreams, learned more practical, domestic tasks, but she had never forgot those dreams. She thought that marriage would renew them, but it was soon apparent that she was required to be the more sensible one, while Morris was able to lose himself in Talmudic study to the exclusion of everything else. She finally realized that neither learning nor romance put food on the table.

She never expected to be so affected by anyone, certainly not so soon after Morris's death. Just thinking about Vaselik made her blush, her legs wobble like a baby trying to take its first step. There was no denying how strongly she felt, but she had never felt at ease discussing these feelings with any other woman. Perhaps they were wrong, even sinful. Her adored father would be devastated if he knew about Vaselik, he would simply die of a broken heart. Her brothers would be equally horrified. The people of Koritz would surely condemn and ostracize her, yet despite all this, she knew that she had to see Vaselik again. It wasn't just her stubbornness, for the first time she felt she was in possession of her dreams.

But survival required her to marshal all her strength and wits. She went again to see Holstein hoping he had a job for her. But the mill was still not running at full capacity and he only needed a little help putting his accounts in order. Watching her juggle the columns of figures, he couldn't mask his surprise that she was so capable of doing the job. His amazement irritated her.

"Mr. Holstein, surely you realize that it is the women who run the businesses in Koritz," she said trying not to sound annoyed, "while their husbands are off studying the Torah."

He turned red, said nothing more and quietly paid her the promised few kopeks. At home she immediately put one of the kopeks into a jar labeled, YAAKOV AND HIS GRANDFATHER. It was a start.

She became good at prowling for food or work, scouting which villagers needed help in clearing away debris from the wreckage of their houses and, in return, would trade food or wood which she used for cooking. This morning she left early for the village square, a shawl protecting her face against the cold air, hurrying through the cobblestone alleys, passing houses in various states of disrepair, which looked so forlorn under the icy-white sun.

Today was the first full-fledged market day since the attack and several women had gathered at one side of the square, their baskets at their feet, containing a few potatoes, dregs of grain and some battered kitchen wares. A few peasants straggled in from the countryside, but their wagons were only half-full with produce.

Leah shifted Joseph to her other shoulder and sent Benny to scout and see if there was anything good to barter with her chicken and a few healthy-looking potatoes. She had high hopes for the future of the two baby chicks at home, but always in the back of her mind, like a miser hiding gold, were the family silver cup and spice box still safe in their hiding place.

After making a tour of the square, Benny reported back, "There are some peasants with fresh vegetables."

In the past when she tried trading with them, they always insisted on cash. "Stay here with Joseph," she said to Benny. "I'll try my luck."

Even with the occasional food parcels brought by Sasha, finding food was a continual game with Leah figuring out who had what, where it was and how she could get it. On a good day, she might trade one egg for a small container of milk, then churn some of the milk into butter, divide the butter in half, and trade again for vegetables. Today did not look to be so lucky.

She walked by slowly, looking out of the corner of her eye at some produce belonging to a heavy-set, peasant woman, also pretending disinterest. Finally, Leah returned and poked through the basket, picking out one small head of cabbage, a bunch of carrots and a firm onion. "I have some potatoes I could trade."

"No trade, cash only," the woman replied, her mouth set in a hard, unyielding line.

Leah considered her options. "Three kopeks," she finally said.

"Four," the woman countered quickly.

"Three," Leah repeated, prepared to leave if the peasant did not relent.

"Okay, okay. You Jews will kill us all with your bargaining."

"You want the sale or not?" Leah was in no mood for insults from this unpleasant old woman. But then she observed the deeply etched lines in the woman's face, how thin her jacket was on this wintry day and the exhausted slump of her shoulders. Leah realized that they both were equals in the world of poverty.

Besides food, she needed to find seeds to plant and a little grain to feed those two baby chicks. Benny had declared himself their guardian, following them everywhere to make sure they didn't escape or get stolen.

Sometimes even in the midst of all this daily game-playing, she would suddenly think of Vaselik, wonder where he was, why she hadn't seen him. The more she tried to forget about him, the more vivid he became. Today she acknowledged that she might never see him again and the thought brought her to tears.

Benny saw her crying and assumed that she must be grieving for Morris. "Do you miss Papa like I do?"

"Yes, of course," she answered, feeling guiltier than ever.

They went home, and Leah set Joseph on a blanket in the kitchen, watching him crawl toward the leg of the table, determined to pull himself upright.

"Benny, come quickly. Look, Joseph is standing." The baby wavered for a few seconds before he realized that he was indeed standing and it so startled him that he immediately let go. As he bounced down onto the floor, he began to cry.

"No *shayna punim*," she said. "Get right back up." She took his two hands, wrapped his fingers around the table leg, so he could keep himself upright. The most important thing for her had to be seeing her boys grow up, not reacting like some romantic schoolgirl, still obsessed with her fantasies.

***

Vaselik sat at his desk, ignoring the recruit who entered his office. He said nothing for a minute or two, wanting the soldier to squirm a bit before he even acknowledged him. The latest recruits that were being sent to him seemed to have come from the riffraff of society; just one step up from criminals. Yet Vaselik's superiors expected him to turn these creatures into soldiers, adhering to military discipline. He could endure the soldiers' occasional creative schemes, but out and out theft would not be tolerated. If they got away with that, they might try more dangerous, mutinous actions. In addition, Vaselik was responsible for overseeing the regimental accounts, which he considered to be beneath him, as if he were some tradesman. He was running out of excuses to explain why he was always over-budget for food supplies.

And this lowly recruit had had the audacity to question Sasha about the food parcels he took to Leah and her children. He couldn't explain his fascination with that woman, except that he was transfixed by those rare occasions when she smiled.

The recruit, Pytor Smirnoff, didn't try to conceal his animosity, still smarting from being called into the captain's office like a small boy being reprimanded by the school principal. He relaxed his stance to express his disdain.

"Stand at attention," Vaseilik snapped angrily. "Stealing is no casual matter and then selling the supplies makes it doubly criminal."

The boy quickly straightened, but replied slyly, "Everybody else seemed to be doing it. Even your orderly."

"Ah, so you're the one making false accusations? Another transgression to add to your record." Despite his disgust with this soldier, Vaselik felt compelled to respond to the charge. "For your information, Smirnoff, and be sure to spread the truth with the same zeal as you did the gossip, those parcels of food were payments to the Widow for her services here, which we terminated in order to accommodate the budget."

Irritated by the show of disbelief displayed on the boy's face, as his jaw slackened and his mouth dropped, Vaselik continued. "You will be on extra duty for the next two weeks, with reduced rations. If I find anyone slipping you even an extra crust of bread, you both will be sent to the brig, dishonorably discharged, a disgrace to your family and Mother Russia. Understand?"

Private Smirnoff nodded, the color draining from his face. "Now get out of my sight." Vaselik hoped he had successfully squelched any ideas of rebellion that might be roiling about in the ranks. If respect didn't command their attention, perhaps fear would.

Vaselik went straight to the stables, anxious for his morning ride. These days only when he rode Nicademus, feeling the flanks of the horse beneath him, did he have any control over his life. He and the horse had perfect communication, like a twentieth century centaur. He thought about his early army days, before all this current military pettiness, wishing he could relive his wild escapades again. As he galloped through the fields, Nicodemus churning up clumps of dirt, Vaselik laughed out loud at the memory of those wild interludes: the all-night drinking sprees, betting large amounts of money, gambling his future on the turn of a card.

How cocky he had been in the gambling halls of Moscow, standing at the table, plunking down his last rubles, tucking one in the décolletage of the charming lady standing next to him, outraging her escort, laughing at the man's distress, Vaselik knew he would never be challenged to a duel, his reputation having proceeded him. Now here in Koritz, he was being suffocated as surely as if he were in quicksand.

A cold wind whipped against his face, the snowy fields stretching before him, a crystal blanket sparkling in the winter sunlight. Bare-branched-trees stood outlined against the sky like neo-classical columns stretching towards the heavens. Further down the road, he spied the outline of a small figure moving slowly, a dark dot against the white snow. He recognized Leah, appearing almost as if he had conjured her, walking alone, for once without her children clinging to her.

He called out, "Good morning." For a moment he thought that she looked almost happy to see him. "I've never seen you out without your children," he said. "I hope they are well."

"Yes," she answered. "They're home, while I visit the old healer, Freydel."

He noticed her shoes were soaked by the snow. "It's very cold and you're wet," he said. "Let me give you a ride to her house." Without waiting for an answer, he bent down and lifted Leah onto his saddle. She did not weigh much, but as he clasped her around the waist he was surprised at how strong her body felt.

Leah started to protest, but she was grateful to be out of the cold slush. As the horse cantered along, she couldn't avoid bumping against Vaselik and when she shivered, he pulled her closer, wrapping her inside his coat. She was acutely aware of his warm breath on the back of her neck, which made her tremble even more, but he assumed it was the cold and bound her even more tightly in his coat.

Near Freydel's house, he stopped, but didn't dismount. "This game we play, it's all nonsense you know," he said.

"Maybe for you it's a game, but for me it's very dangerous." Even as affected as she was in his presence, she couldn't stop from speaking sharply.

He got off the horse, lifted Leah down, but held onto her bare hands, blowing on them to warm them. Her face reddened and she tried to pull back, but he didn't let go.

"It eludes me why I should be so interested, when you're so resistant." He searched her face for any sign of feeling, even a glimpse of the pleasure he imagined he saw before.

"What you mean to say, is how surprising that you could be interested in a Jew who dares to refuse you."

"Stop it. What I mean to say, is what I already did say. Just once, show me that tender side you exhibit when you look at your children." He wrapped his coat around her and pulled her closer. "You must know I would never harm you," Vaselik whispered, cupping her face, as he gently kissed her eyelids.

His unexpected gentleness confounded her, evaporating all her resistance and she lifted her face to meet his kiss, her mouth on his. "I know this must be wrong," she whispered, but clasped him even more tightly.

"Come see me tonight," he said. "The Widow Popov is away visiting her daughter in the next village, so no one will see you."

"No, you can't be serious." Succumbing to his kiss was an act of rashness, but it would be madness to continue any further and yet…

He still held her face in his hands, her cheeks burning in the icy chill.

"Yes, I'm very serious," he said. "Don't say anything more. I'll wait for you tonight."

Leah went inside to see Freydel, but she appeared so distracted that Freydel asked if she were unwell. She was seconds away from confiding in the old woman, but years of keeping her thoughts to herself made her wary, certain that this was not the time to reveal her attraction to a Russian officer. As much as Freydel liked Leah, a confession like that would certainly end any friendship between them. Instead Leah sat quietly, drinking the ginger tea that Freydel had brewed for her, staring into the fireplace. All she desired, she told herself, was a quiet life, allowed to simply raise her children.

Freydel brought out some new herbs, expecting to teach Leah how to grow and use them, but Leah had no concentration. She begged off, asking to come back another day. On the way home Leah told herself that of course she couldn't see Vaselik, but an inner voice challenged her. Life was giving her a chance now to take a risk or forever stay cautious.

That evening, after she fed the children, Leah decided that she had to go and detail to Vaselik how impossible this whole situation was. Although she was so taken with him, she was frightened at the consequences. She bundled Joseph and Benny in warm clothes and explained to Benny that she was going to talk to the Captain about possible work. She decided that taking the children would be her shield from continuing this insanity.

"Mama, I could watch Joseph at home while you're gone." The boy was not enthusiastic about getting dressed and going out into the night air. "I'm big enough to take care of him for a little while."

"I know you are, sweetheart, but I don't like leaving you alone, especially after dark. The Widow won't be there and you'll like snuggling under her big goose down quilt. And if you're good, I have a treat for you."

Vaselik heard Leah knock softly at the door, surprised that she came, even though he had been sitting expectantly for nearly two hours. He showed none of his usual swagger as he opened the door, acting more like a hopeful suitor, then he realized that Leah had brought her children.

"I told Benny that he could rest in the Widow's bed," she said, going straight to the bedroom. She spread a shawl across the bed, tucked the children under the quilt, then took out a slice of bread with the raspberry preserves that Benny liked so much. He eagerly ate it, being careful not to drop crumbs on the sheets, while she constructed a barrier of chairs on the side of the bed so Joseph could not tumble off.

When she returned to the sitting room, Vaselik stood, his back to the fireplace. "I've wanted to do this for a long time," he said and reached over to untie the scarf that covered her head. He stared as if seeing her for the first time, her face glowing in the firelight, her hair reflecting glints of reddish gold.

Without the scarf Leah felt almost undressed, but more like a young girl again. No one but Morris had seen her bareheaded since her wedding day. She blushed and put her hands up to cover her braids, but Vaselik unbraided them so her hair fell loose about her shoulders. He offered her some wine, but its heady aroma was so unlike the sweet Shabbos wine that she was used to that she refused.

"It's a pity to cover such loveliness," he said. He reached out again to touch her hair, but Leah drew back, trying to remember all the reasons she shouldn't stay, the ones that she had planned to tell him. She even thought of Tolstoy's *Anna Karenina* but the tragic ending of that romance frightened her even more. Still, she didn't resist when Vaselik kissed her.

"No more," she said, breathless, sinking onto the chaise. She re-tied her scarf, using the time to calm her pounding heart. "I should leave. I only came this evening to tell you why we must never meet again, but I feel almost bewitched."

"It is I who am under a spell," he said. "I've never allowed anyone to come close to me and then I let you pierce my heart with those eyes of yours."

He sat next to her and slowly laced his fingers with hers. Leah shivered as the fire burned itself out and Vaselik put his arm around her shoulders. Staying was dangerous, but she made no effort to leave when he brushed his lips lightly across the palm of her hand. Nothing would ever be the same if she stayed. And still, she did not leave. Even her children sleeping in the next room, whom she brought as a shield, a reminder to her conscience, did not move her.

"Tonight must be our secret," she said to him. "Swear it."

Vaselik was startled by her wish to keep their meeting hidden, even though he realized that they both faced censure if anyone learned about this evening.

"Of course I swear," he said. Your children are sleeping, the Widow is away, when will there be such an opportunity again to be alone."

He kissed her neck, then slowly began to unbutton her dress, one hand sliding inside her bodice caressing her skin, the other hand moving down along her hip, lifting the hem of her skirt, slipping in between her thighs. There was no rush to his movements, Vaselik savored looking at her as much as touching her. Leah felt she was floating in space, as if time had stopped and the earth was falling off its axis. For once she was unable to separate the real from the dream.

The room glowed in the blurry light from the fireplace. She had no thoughts of wanting to resist. Vaselik's face was so close, his breath warm, his arms holding her tightly. His touch made her feel as if she had drunk too much potent wine. Even though she wanted to see herself reflected in his eyes, she hesitated to open her own eyes, afraid that Vaselik, the room, everything, might disappear. When at last he entered inside her, the surge of delight was almost too much to bear.

She heard him whisper, "I'm always yours, if you want me." She wanted this moment to last forever.

chapter 15

BEFORE THE FIRST light of dawn, Leah tiptoed into the Widow's bedroom and lay down next to Benny. The boy slept deeply. She was happy to see that he wasn't restlessly turning or nightmare whimpering in his sleep. Here in the Widow's house, lying on a thick mattress stuffed with soft goose feathers, he was at last enjoying his best sleep since the attack. But she still felt selfish at having dragged him and Joseph out tonight.

Perhaps it was insanity or simply Vaselik's charm that bewitched her into sleeping with him, but tonight she had experienced sensations of delight unknown to her before. She never thought that she was capable of feeling such physical pleasure, that it had always been her fault that her relationship with Morris was so unfulfilled. But what now? The liason with Vaselik frightened her. Yet she cared for this man in ways more than merely physical. Yes he was charming, but difficult, compassionate but sometimes inflexible. Unlike anyone she had ever known. Was she endangering the lives of her children for her own pleasure?

She remembered the day she came to Koritz. Morris was waiting for her carriage to arrive, ready to go immediately to the Rebbe's house for the wedding ceremony. They had met once during the matchmaking when he had travelled to Yanoff. She thought he looked scholarly, his beard neatly trimmed, his demeanor shy and unprepossessing.

Neighbors had left food for their supper. "You don't want to start cooking on your wedding night," the Rebbe's wife told her. Morris blushed and Leah, tired from her long journey, was anxious to see her new home.

Morris took her suitcase and they walked home, Leah clutching the Ketuba, their Jewish marriage license.

A few village women stood outside the house to greet them. "May you be blessed with long life and many sons," Yetta Weiss said, handing Leah one of her husband's freshly baked breads and a cup of salt as an offering for the couple's new life. They all admired Leah's dress, her only new expenditure for the occasion, observing, "Velvet inserts, very grand." That dress had stayed packed away until the attack burned down the house.

Yetta had whispered into Leah's ear, "We put a mezuzah, once blessed by Rebbe Nachman himself, on your door. You'll be having sons before you know it."

Haim Holstein arrived bringing wine and toasted Leah and Morris. "Here's to our happy couple." Leon Lipski gave them a pitcher of fresh milk from his finest cow and then started to play his fiddle, slowly at first, but building to a riotous, joyous climax. Like a Pied Piper, he led the villagers away, playing a lilting Chassidic melody that lingered in the air as they all followed him into the night.

Morris took Leah into the house, just one large room separated into two areas by a curtain strung across the space. Neither of them were particularly hungry so she put her things away in the bedroom, changed into a night shift, brushed out her hair and sat on the bed waiting for Morris. She could hear him recite his prayers in the other room. Remembering the beautiful affection that her parents had shared she waited in great anticipation.

He blew out the candle and slipped into bed. They lay side by side for a long time in the dark, before he turned and awkwardly climbed on top of her. Without a word, he pushed himself inside her, completing his wedding-night duties quickly with a soft moan, then rolled off and said goodnight, before reciting a final prayer, then fell asleep. Leah lay in the dark saying her own fervent prayer that tomorrow might be different.

Now she felt it was imperative to leave before Vaselik awoke. She roused Benny and Joseph, quickly dressed them and hurried from the house. As they briskly walked home, the cold temperatures helped to clear her brain and she wondered what price she would have to pay for her pleasure. Her world believed that that a woman's reward came only through marriage and children. Sexual pleasure was never even mentioned. And a liaison with a Russian officer could bring down the wrath of the community unless it was somehow kept secret. Surprisingly, she didn't feel sinful, just a bit dishonest. She might rate high on the list of sinners, but Leah knew that in Koritz, like everywhere else, there were many who had their own secrets, ones they would not want revealed to man or God. Even the noble Mr. Holstein had his share of rumors about dalliances with women not his wife. But of course he was a man and could be forgiven his mistakes.

When they finally arrived home, Leah saw Yaakov's horse and wagon parked out in front, Yaakov stretched out asleep on the seat, while Drushka pawed the ground hoping to find buried shoots of grass to eat.

"Yaakov, wake up. You'll freeze to death out here. Come in." They all went inside, Leah settling the children close to the hearth, while she lit a fire. Then she took Joseph into the bedroom to clean and nurse him. When she came back out Yaakov had stoked the fire with more wood and filled the samovar to brew tea. She was thankful that he didn't ask any questions as to why she had been out so early in the morning.

Instead he brought out some cookies which he had in his pocket. "A treat for Benny," he said, offering them to the boy. "And this is for Joseph," dangling a small rag doll, which the baby immediately put into his mouth.

"What do you say, Benny?" Leah asked the boy as she heated a pot of kasha, stirring in a little milk.

"Can I eat them now?" Benny asked eagerly.

"First, thank Yaakov. You may have one now, save the rest for later."

The boy blushed at his greediness, shyly saying "Thank you, Yaakov."

"And for you, Leah, I also have a gift." From another pocket, Yaakov emptied a packet of seeds into Leah's palm. "The beginnings of your new vegetable garden, although the woman who gave them to me couldn't remember which vegetables they were," he said, laughing.

"You have been so good to us." She brought down the jar with its label YAAKOV AND GRANDFATHER. "This is my *pishka*," she said, referring to the special container every Jewish family used to collect money for the poor. "I have already put in a few kopeks to repay you."

He brushed the hair out of his eyes, plopping down cross-legged in front of the fire. "Someday when I need help," he said, "I'm sure I'll be able to count on you." He didn't look at Leah directly, suddenly looking like a shy young schoolboy, awkwardly expressing his feelings. "And of course you, too, Benny." He lightly punched Benny on the shoulder, but the boy was too engrossed in his cookie to respond.

"We're having another meeting tonight, if you can come," Yaakov said. "Someone from Moscow will be speaking to us."

"The soldiers are watching the village very closely," she said, speaking in a whisper, even though they were inside. "They are on the lookout for anyone who might be involved in organizing."

"We're all very careful. I'm a peddler, no one suspects anything when I move around. And so far we haven't had anyone from Koritz attending."

"Except for me, of course." She picked up Joseph, holding him as if he were her shield against all problems, but he squirmed out of her grasp to get down and play with his doll.

"Nothing will change in this country without taking some risks, but if you're nervous, I won't press you." Yaakov sounded disappointed as he reached over to distract the crying baby by dangling the doll in front of him.

"I'm a mother first, Yaakov."

She had already jeopardized her children by her relationship with Vaselik, but she couldn't explain that to the boy. Of course she wanted a better life for Benny and Joseph, but would going tonight be one risk too many? Yaakov acted so confident about this meeting, that after a moment, she finally relented. "If you think tonight is alright, I'll go."

Yaakov's face lit up at her change of heart.

He returned after dark to pick up Leah and the boys. It was impossible to leave the children with anyone who might ask questions. Her only option was the same as always, to keep them close to her as she had been doing ever since the night Morris died.

The meeting was held in a different place than the last time, locations rotated, but the house was also off the main road, near the edge of the woods. The room overflowed with people, but she was relieved that she didn't recognize any of them. Yaakov pointed out to her the Jews who lived in nearby villages and towns, as well as those who had traveled all day to attend. There was a mixture of young men, their hands rough and work-worn, men formally dressed in shiny black suits, young women an eager look in their eyes, all anxious according to Yaakov, anxious to find an oasis of action in the middle of a desert of oppression.

"Tonight we're here," the speaker said, standing on a chair in the center of the room, "to push the government to implement the concessions they've agreed to: more religious tolerance, more freedom of speech, the formation of a 'consultative assembly'; all things they've promised but haven't done so far." He never identified himself and looked different from the other men, Leah thought. His hands were soft, with long tapered fingers, but his deep-set eyes burned behind wire-rimmed glasses. "The government thinks they can stop us with their guns, but we won't stop protesting until they listen."

A dark-haired girl, identified only as Anna, jumped up, her voice high-pitched in anger. "Some of you have suffered through the recent attacks, you've lost loved ones, your homes, your livelihood, so you know how important it is now to work with us. If we stand together, we can win." Her skin was shiny with perspiration, her hands balled into fists, punching the air, punctuating her words like tiny hammers.

Her passion energized the room, but one man stood up slowly. He was much older than the others, his face deeply lined from many years of working outdoors in all weather, his hair a thick shock of white.

"Be careful, that's all I have to say. No matter what the authorities promise, don't trust them. If anything goes wrong, they'll blame us Jews. The latest is the failure of the war against the Japanese. They are accusing us of treason and conspiring with the enemy. They mark us like the biblical scapegoat to carry all their sins."

Arguments continued in all corners of the room, some debated the merits of holding onto the traditions of religion versus the more secular rewards of life. Others worried about the harsh reprisals. One man, who had been a witness to government reprisals on Bloody Sunday, vehemently warned, "Anyone involved in advancing reforms or revolution against the government, could face prison or a firing squad." The discussions raged on past midnight, when Leah decided it was time to leave and asked Yaakov to return home. He left the conversation reluctantly, picking up the sleeping Benny while she carried Joseph.

Leah understood that Yaakov was right; freedom was as important to their welfare as getting enough food to eat. If Russia didn't change, how could her children ever have a better life? Even though the government had emancipated the serfs, they had made sure they had no political or economic power to go along with that mandate, leaving the peasants poor and frustrated, blaming not only the government, but the Jews for all their troubles. With the monarchy's power remaining absolute, how could any of them make a difference? Yet the one thing that Judaism had taught her, if you save one life, it's as if you've saved the whole world.

It was very late when they arrived home and there at the front door was a large package, filled to the top with eggs, a bag of flour, potatoes, carrots, a canister of milk, salt, onions, apples and a jar of cherry preserves. She recognized the handwriting on the unsigned, attached note, which asked "Why did you leave while I was asleep?" Leah grabbed the note before Yaakov had a chance to see it.

"Well, it looks as if you have a guardian angel," he said, eyeing the contents of the basket.

Leah's cheeks burned in embarrassment, but felt obliged to say something. "No, it's just in exchange for cooking at the barracks."

"I thought you no longer worked there." Yaakov looked a little confused by her explanation.

"Yes, that's true. But they still owed me an additional payment."

He helped her carry the children to bed. Benny never opened his eyes as Leah tucked him under the covers, while Joseph stuck his thumb in his mouth and immediately fell asleep.

"Why don't you just curl up next to the fireplace," she said to Yaakov. "It's too late to ride off tonight."

"No thanks," he said. "If I leave now, I'll make the next town by early morning. I can doze while I'm riding." He watered his horse and left.

In the morning after the children had their breakfast, Leah put Benny in charge of Joseph, explaining that she'd be back in a very short while. It was the first time she was leaving them alone and she wanted to complete her errand quickly. She intended to return the food basket to Vaselik at his office, transporting it in a wheelbarrow. On the way, she passed a couple of villagers and simply nodded and continued on to the barracks.

Outside Vaselik's office, she greeted Sasha, requesting a minute with the Captain.

Vaselik stood at the window, his back towards her, as she entered the office. She had planned to stay in control, but immediately, her heart beat faster at the sight of the broad shoulders, the straight back.

"I'm returning the food," Leah said.

He didn't turn around, but stiffened noticeably. "Why are you always so difficult?" he sighed. "I just want to help you."

"It feels like a payment. It's insulting."

Vaselik walked over to her and took her hands. "You are an impossible woman, but you must keep the food. It's too absurd otherwise."

"This situation is absurd. I don't know how to act. It is unnerving." He kept holding her hands, making it difficult for her to continue.

"Let me help when I can," he said. "Why is that so hard to accept?"

"Because we're on opposite sides. And I can't forget that."

"You were able to forget for a little while, Leah. Why can't you separate those problems from us?" His voice softened. "Come again tonight. I'll find a way to get rid of the Widow."

"No. I can't."

"Then I'll come to see you," he said. "We can't talk here. Now take the food and enjoy it, please."

Her arguments sounded lame and she began to feel foolish, so she returned home with the food, but kept it covered so no one could see it.

That night she put the boys to sleep and sat by the fire, nervously sipping a glass of tea, when she heard a light tap at the door. Taking a deep breath, she concentrated on putting one foot in front of the other, opening the door to Vaselik.

He carried a small bottle, two glasses and a tin of cookies. "I knew you wouldn't have any brandy and I thought you might enjoy some sweets. Before you start lecturing me, this is just a gesture of friendship."

"Where did you leave your horse?" It would take just one inquisitive neighbor to start trouble.

"I tied him up in the back. No one will spot him, I promise."

"You don't understand the awkward position I'm in. I have no family here to support me. My neighbors' good will is important."

"Do you really care that much about the neighbors?" he asked, pouring out some brandy in the two glasses.

"I do for the boys' sakes, if not my own."

He sat down next to her and untied her scarf, pushing her hands out of the way, loosening her hair, combing through it with his fingers. "If only I could see you dressed as you should be, just once."

"I'm not someone to be dressed and painted like one of your fancy women."

"More's the pity. Did you always argue with your husband over every word he said?" He laughed and the sound startled Leah, she realized that it was the first time she had ever heard him laugh. "You would have made a good soldier," he said, "always on the attack."

She smiled. "My father used to call me his little general."

That time was so long ago. Barely thirteen when her mother took ill, she had the responsibility of running the household. As much as she grieved for her mother, she had loved the opportunity of being in charge of her adored father and brothers. She could not understand why they hadn't answered her letters.

Vaselik saw a hairbrush on the table and began to brush her hair, with long, languid strokes. Each stroke felt like a caress, both embarrassing her and exciting her. In ten years of marriage, she could not remember Morris ever touching her hair. He was the only man permitted to see it uncovered, yet he always acted as if it was wicked to watch her comb or braid it. If he had loved looking at her, he was never able to express it. When Vaselik replaced the brush on the table he saw the book of Pushkin poems that Yaakov's grandfather had sent her. "You like his poetry?"

He turned the pages and found the poem, *Remembrence,* reciting a few lines:

Dreams seethe; and fretful infelicities
Are swarming in my over-burdened soul,
And Memory before my wakeful eyes.
With noiseless hand unwinds her lengthy scroll.

Vaselik handed the book to Leah so she could continue reading.

With loathing I peruse the years,
I tremble, and I curse my natal day,
Wail bitterly and bitterly shed tears,
But cannot wash the woeful script away.

"Such a melancholy thought," she said. "I favor his more romantic poems."

Vaselik regarded her with a new respect. "I do understand your fear," he said, "but I must see you again, if you will let me."

"I worry about my boys. But...,"then she stopped, leaving the rest of her thoughts unspoken.

He lightly kissed the top of her head and she leaned into his chest, feeling the rough material of his uniform against her cheek, breathing in the pungent mixture of brandy and tobacco, amazed by the poetic side that he had revealed to her.

But then he was gone and she was left sitting by the dying fire, alone with her thoughts and her dreams.

chapter 16

EVEN THOUGH LEAH was not always successful at healing her neighbors with her herbs and poultices, they still came when their children fell sick in hopes that she could help them. She had the best results with colic, simple fevers, sprains or congestion from a cold and in return, they repaid her with whatever they could spare: an egg, some potatoes, grain, a pitcher of milk. But what would happen if someone was really ill, like the time Joseph hovered near death. It gave her shivers when she remembered how powerless she had been, it was Vaselik who helped save him.

The calls continued with the cold and rainy weather, so when there was an urgent knock late one night, Leah expected to see an anxious, upset neighbor. Instead a young girl, perhaps twenty, stood in the doorway, drenched by the driving rain, water pooling at her feet, as she looked around nervously like a hunted rabbit.

"Yaakov said you might help me," she whispered. "My name is Sarah."

"Are you sick?" Leah asked, wondering why Yaakov would send a stranger to her for medical help. He knew she wasn't that experienced.

"Not exactly. May I come in, please?" Since the girl was clearly in distress, Leah ushered her inside.

"Is anyone else here?" Sarah looked around, her frightened eyes searching, her body trembling.

"Just my children. Why?" The girl's fear was obvious, so Leah tried to put her at ease. "Sit by the fire to warm yourself. I'll get you some hot tea."

Leah put more sticks of wood on the fire and poured a glass of tea, looking closer at the shivering girl. Sarah's shoes were caked with mud; her coat rain-soaked, strands of hair were plastered to her face, even though her head and shoulders had been covered by a heavy shawl.

"Now tell me why Yaakov sent you." The lateness of the hour and Sarah's nervousness made Leah uneasy, even though the girl looked somewhat familiar.

"I'm part of the Bund that Yaakov belongs to. I saw you with him at our last meeting." Sarah removed her coat and shawl and slipped off her shoes, spreading them out on the hearth to dry, then picked up the tea, warming her hands on the glass, holding it close to her face.

"Some of the members and I began to suspect that one of our leaders might be under surveillance because of our work and we decided it was safer to split up and disperse. Yaakov hoped you might let me stay here for a day or two. He would have come himself to ask, but he was driving one of the other older men to another place and could only drop me close to Koritz. I walked the rest of the way."

"What is he thinking? He knows I have young children. How can he ask me to put them in danger?" Leah was surprised by this imposition. She refilled the glass for the still-shivering girl.

"I won't put you out at this hour, but at first light you have to go."

"Of course, I understand." Tears of exhaustion flooded Sarah's eyes as she nodded. "I just need a little time to sleep and dry out," she said. "But I swear to you, I haven't actually seen anyone watching me."

"Yet you're here trembling with fear."

Leah brought out some dark bread slathered with cherry preserves. She remembered the brandy that Vaselik had left behind, and poured a little into the girl's tea.

"If my boy Benny wakes up, tell him you are an old childhood friend of mine. Don't mention Yaakov. The less Benny knows the better."

The girl hungrily finished the bread and jam and swallowed the fortified tea quickly, repeating, "I'm sorry to cause you any inconvenience." She curled up near the fireplace, covering herself with a shawl that Leah brought, wrapping it around her.

"You have to take off that wet dress," Leah said. "I'll get you something else to put on." She found a cotton shift for Sarah to wear and once wrapped in the warm shawl the girl fell asleep instantly.

Leah returned to bed, praying that none of her neighbors would make a sick call before Sarah left. She heard Benny snuffling in his sleep next to her, but she was too nervous to sleep, staying awake, alert to any strange noises outside, terrified that Sarah had been followed. Despite her fear and irritation at the imposition, Leah had to admire the girl's courage. Since the attack, Leah realized how difficult it was to be brave, to take risks in the face of danger. Events moved so fast, you couldn't be sure that what you were doing was the right thing. That moment when she appealed to the young soldier had been a test, but she didn't know if she could ever be that brave again.

At first light, Leah awoke to find Sarah up and already dressed. The rain continued to come down in sheets and the girl hesitated at the door.

"Wait," Leah called. "Have something to eat first."

Sara looked relieved. "Thank you. If I could just stay a little longer, perhaps the rain will stop."

Benny came into the kitchen pulling on a sweater. "Mama, I left the buckets outside last night, so they would get filled with rainwater." He looked surprised seeing Sarah, his face a small question mark.

"Benny, this is Sarah. A friend from Yanoff, someone I knew a long time ago." Benny and Joseph had dozed during the last meeting Yaakov took them to, so there was no chance that he would recognize her. The boy seemed content with Leah's explanation and did not ask any questions, but Leah felt it necessary to add, "She was on her way to Zvil and stopped here to visit a little. But the weather was so bad I made her spend the night."

She clung to the belief that no one in Koritz would deliberately turn in another Jew, but on the chance that anyone questioned Benny, she wanted to be sure that he had the right answers. Just one wrong word to the military could have bad consequences.

"Benny, check the shed and see if the chicken laid any more eggs."

The boy grabbed some stale bread from the table, pulled his sweater up around his head and darted out quickly, flying over mud puddles which were laid out like path of pebbles between their place and the shed. The bird rested on a mound of hay and allowed him to reach underneath and carefully extract a beautiful egg which he sheltered inside his shirt. But Benny didn't see or hear his baby chicks. He checked every inch of the space, becoming frantic when he spied a crack in the wooden door that had been pecked at repeatedly, enlarging the opening. Outside, he saw the two chicks lying next to each other, stiff and dead in the mud.

Benny ran back to the kitchen, splashing right through the puddles, shouting, "Mama, come quick." He pulled her outside and pointed to the lifeless chicks, too choked with grief to say anything more, his little chest heaving with sobs.

Leah wrapped her arms around him, trying to lead him indoors. "No," he yelled, pushing her away. "I have to bury them."

"You're soaked," she said. "I don't want you to get sick."

Damn you God! Give a child a little joy and then snatch it away from him. She insisted, "Benny, come inside, **now**." But he ran to the chicks. She picked him up and almost threw him into the shed. "I'll bury them," she said. "You stay there."

She carried the two little birds, ignoring the torrents of rain and dug a hole in the muddy ground with her fingers, under the outcropping of the shed roof. Then gently laying the birds on a flat rock at the bottom of the hole, she quickly filled it in with more dirt before water flooded it, marking the spot with another two large stones. She tried to console Benny, who struggled against her so furiously that the egg still sheltered in his shirt was smashed. Finally, he allowed her to take him indoors.

In the house, he hiccoughed between sobs. "I'm sorry, Mama. I should have taken better care of them."

"They were just too curious for their own good." She cleaned the oozing yolk from his sweater. "I'm afraid it will only be tea with bread and jam for breakfast," she said to Sarah.

"I have a surprise for you," Sarah said, reaching into her satchel. She brought out two shiny red apples. "I had almost forgotten about them. Yaakov sent them."

"Wonderful," Leah said. She peeled them and gave them to Benny and Sarah, saving a piece for Joseph to gnaw on. "You have to stay until the rain stops," she told Sarah. "I'd feel terrible if you get sick because of me. I'll pack some soup and bread for you to take with you."

A loud knock at the door startled them. Leah cautiously asked "Who is it?" A muffled voice answered, "It's me, Yaakov." She opened the door to see an unusually nervous-looking Yaakov, standing there rain-soaked.

"I thought since I was passing nearby, I'd stop to make sure everything is alright."

Leah indicated that she wanted to speak to him privately. They walked into the bedroom.

"Truthfully, Yaakov, things are not really alright. My house is not be the safest place to hide people," she said, pacing back and forth, her voice sounding harsh and strident.

"Why?" he asked, looking a little perplexed.

"Because even though I stopped working for the army, the captain's orderly stops by frequently to check on the children." She spoke the truth, but left out any details about Vaselik's visits.

"Exactly why your place is perfect. We 're not sure that anyone is actually looking for Sarah and if you're a friend of this orderly no one would ever suspect that you would be harboring anyone." As he spoke, Yaakov emptied a bag containing potatoes, carrots, onions and two eggs, carefully wrapped in heavy cotton cloth.

"You think a few eggs will make up for the danger you've put my children in?"

Today, Yaakov's gifts disturbed Leah. Did everyone think that a handout of food was all it took to win her over? That she was someone who was willing to cooperate as long as she got paid.

"I'm sorry but yours was the nearest house I could think of for Sarah. If you're upset, I won't do it again."

He looked so contrite that Leah began to feel guilty. "I do want to help," she said. "But my situation is precarious."

Then Leah heard Gittel call through the door, "Are you home Leah? Yussel is sick."

Leah put her finger to her lips. "You and Sarah are just visiting," she whispered. "Let me do the explanations."

She opened the door and Gittel entered, carrying Yussel, who was a little younger than Benny. "He has a fever and coughed and wheezed all night." Gittel laid him on the kitchen table, then noticed Yaakov and Sarah.

"It's a bit early in the day for you isn't it, Yaakov?" Even though Gittel addressed Yaakov, she looked directly at Sarah.

Leah intervened, "Sarah is an old family friend who lived near me in Yanoff and Yaakov agreed to give her a ride." She immediately turned to Yussel. "Does anything hurt you?" The child shook his head. "Let me see your throat." The boy opened his mouth wide, then doubled over with a dry, hacking cough.

Checking through the satchel, Leah found some sprigs of hyssop and chamomile flowers which she gave to Gittel. "Brew these into a tea for Yussel three times a day. That should bring down the fever and help the cough."

Gittel looked relieved. "Thank you, Leah. When I buy milk later today, I'll get some for you."

Leah always worried whether she had made the right choice. She could never forget the baby who died despite her efforts and sometimes she thought that her patients would have gotten better left on their own. Still, the tea would certainly ease Yussel's cough and she would be happy to have the milk. Being paid for her efforts at healing seemed fair enough.

When the rain finally stopped, Yaakov and Sarah left to find another safe place for the girl. Leah wondered if Yaakov told the truth about no one tracking Sarah. For someone who was not in danger, he seemed determined to keep moving her about.

"Mama, is Sarah really an old friend of yours?" Benny came into the kitchen, a concerned look on his face. At times like this, his serious expressions always reminded her of Morris.

"Why do you ask?" Joseph finished nursing and lay quietly asleep in her arms, a trace of a smile on his face, as sweet and fresh as a morning sky.

"She acted so scared, not like any of the other friends who used to come here."

"These are different times, Benny. People have reason to be scared. Look what happened here in Koritz."

She hated to keep alarming him, but even at eight, it was important to always be aware of his circumstances. Her brothers and she had also grown up hearing scary stories about how young boys, sometimes as young as Benny, had been kidnapped by the army, hauled off to serve a twenty-five year enlistment and physically coerced to convert to Russian Orthodoxy.

Neighbors were known to sometimes alert the kidnappers about other boys, in order to save their own sons.

"Sarah is a young girl, all on her own, so of course she'd be scared. But you don't have to worry, because you have me to protect you."

"But Mama, I should protect you. I'm the man of the house."

So serious, Leah thought, just like his father. He's growing up much too quickly.

That afternoon Sasha came by with a request that she cook for the Captain the next evening. "I believe it is the Captain's twentieth anniversary in the military and he wishes to have something special to commemorate the occasion."

Sasha was so formal, as if he were announcing a great event, but she saw a glimmer of a smile lurking behind his eyes, making her wonder whether he was laughing at her or Vaselik. Did he guess by now that there was some sort of special connection between her and his captain?

"As long as I can bring my children, I can do it," she said.

"Perhaps you would allow me to take care of Benny. He could stay with me and I'd bring him home in the morning."

Even though it was Sasha, she'd never agree to leave the children alone with any Russian soldier, never. "No," she said emphatically," the boys stay close to me or I cannot come."

"I'll tell the captain, Missus." He looked disappointed, returning later to say that Captain Vaselik would expect her the next day, with the boys, at the Widow Popov's, ready to cook by five o'clock.

The following day the Widow opened the back door for Leah and the children and sullenly showed them to a small room next to the kitchen. It was bare of all furniture except for a small bed where Benny and Joseph would be allowed to rest.

"The captain told me you had to bring your children again. All of this is too much commotion for me, so I am going off to visit my daughter. Do not touch anything else in the house."

The woman's manner has not improved, Leah thought looking through the dinner ingredients that Sasha had left. With an attitude like that, the Widow could certainly stir up trouble in the village; although Leah's Jewish neighbors would be less likely to be impressed with anything she said. But if she suspected that Leah was having a relationship with Vaselik, her jealousy could be dangerous.

As she unpacked the food, Leah found a note tucked inside which read, "Cook dinner for two and please wear the grey dress, with no arguments. Tonight is my anniversary and I do not wish to be bothered with any problems or complaints."

The captain was expected at eight, so she immediately began her preparations, stuffing the chicken with prunes and rice, roasting potatoes in the coals, cooking winter greens with onions and garlic, as well as baking a honey cake dotted with raisins and walnuts. She kept wondering who else the captain was entertaining that night. Perhaps it was one of his military friends, someone who was also celebrating an anniversary. It certainly wasn't the widow, who left to visit her daughter, acting much put upon, as if she had been evicted by force, instead of being paid a handsome sum, which Leah saw Sasha give her before she left.

At the end of the preparations, she changed into the grey dress. It was part of the bargain she had made, so Leah wasn't sure why it disturbed her so much. The dress was of better quality than anything else she owned in years. Perhaps that was why it bothered her, it didn't belong to her, she wouldn't have accepted it, but it emphasized the wide gap that separated Vaselik and her. Even their night of lovemaking hadn't changed that, in fact, it made everything even more apparent.

Vaselik arrived promptly at eight, bearing packages of fruit, wine and candies. He requested that Leah light candles in the formal dining room, set out the Widow's best china and glasses, pour wine into a decanter, then before serving dinner, feed her children and come into the sitting room.

"Aren't you going to wait for your guest?" she asked, beginning to feel a bit uneasy.

Standing by the fireplace, she thought he carried his twenty years in the military lightly. With only a few grey hairs at the temples, he could pass for a hero out of Tolstoy's *War and Peace*.

"There's no one coming," he said smiling. "It's just the two of us."

How did she not see it? Or had she ignored that possibility because then she would have had to refuse the evening. Instead she blindly cooperated and now she was alone with Vaselik.

"Tonight you must have some wine to celebrate my anniversary."

Vaselik poured two glasses, the firelight turning the wine into liquid garnet, the same deep color of a necklace she remembered her mother had once worn. Vaselik stood so close, that she could smell a mixture of tobacco and a whiff of oranges which clung to his clothes.

"Don't say anything," he said, "don't analyze everything. Let me enjoy this moment, my celebration."

It was almost a plea, the kind made by a very young boy, like Benny when he begged to stay under the covers on a cold, winter's morning. She said nothing, relenting to take a sip after they clinked glasses, the sound of the Widow's crystal gently reverberating.

He bent towards her, his lips softly brushing the top of her head, and quietly asked, "Who was the girl who visited you yesterday? A friend of yours or the peddler?"

Leah was taken aback by his question, but tried to answer calmly. "Sarah and her family were friends of my parents. Why?"

"Such a far distance for a young girl to travel by herself, don't you think?" He sat down on the chaise, pulling Leah down with him.

"That's why Yaakov agreed to accompany her the rest of the way as a favor." Why did he care? How did he know so much? Her whole body inwardly screamed.

"Do you know who brought her to Koritz?"

He stared at her, increasing her concern. "No, I never asked. It was bad weather, and I was more interested in getting her dry and warm. But I resent your interrogating me as if I were some criminal. You're talking about friends of mine." She stood up. "I'll serve dinner now, if you're ready." But he wouldn't release her hand.

"Be careful. I'm only concerned for your safety. There are people out there stirring up trouble and it's my duty to find and stop them."

When he finally let go of her hand, she walked into the kitchen, trying not to shake. She checked on the children; saw Benny playing with the carved soldiers that Sasha had made for him and Joseph gnawing away on his rag doll. Joseph was probably getting some new teeth, she thought, forcing herself to remain calm but vigilant.

The more wine Vaselik drank, the more charming and romantic he became, holding Leah's chair for her, praising the meal effusively, kissing her hands in appreciation, then attempting to fold her into his arms, until she swiveled out of his grasp to bring in tea and dessert.

"No, no tea," he insisted. "Some brandy, but in the other room, by the fire."

She had hardly eaten and the little wine that she drank had made her a little lightheaded, which she fought against. This was no time to be tipsy, no time to fall prey to Vaselik's temptations. Somehow he knew who came to her home and considered her visitors to be a possible threat. Even though she knew she mustn't succumb to him again, she longed for his touch as a wave of sadness enveloped her.

Vaselik took a slim leather-bound volume from the mantel and handed it to Leah. "Since you're a lover of poetry, I wanted you to have this book by Fyodor Tyutchev, a most romantic poet."

She opened to a page which was book-marked by a silk ribbon and read aloud:

It's there, still there, a past love's madness,

Dull pain and longing my heart fill.

Your image, hid amid the shadows

Of memory, lives in me still.

She stopped, unable to continue. Vaselik took the book and read:

I think of it with endless yearning,

'Tis e'er with me though from me far,

Unreachable, unchanged, bright-burning

As in the sky of night a star.

"Please" she said, "no more." She rose, began gathering the glasses to take into the kitchen.

"Nothing I say convinces you of my sincere feelings." He stood between her and the door.

"It doesn't matter. Our lives can't intersect anymore." It was less than an hour ago that he had uttered words of warning to her. Now he acted as though she should consider them words of love.

Vaselik bristled at her words, which completely spoiled his evening's festivities. He pulled Leah to him, pressed his mouth against hers, his arms like bands of steel.

"Stop," she cried. "You're frightening me."

His evening had completely soured. He released her and lit a long thin cigar. "You're angry about my questions. Well, that's my responsibility, asking questions, finding out what people are doing."

"Yes of course," she said. "We all have our duty." With that she left the room, went into the room where the children slept and woke Benny. "Come, sweetheart. We are going home."

He looked up at her sleepily. "Mama, what's the matter?"

"I'm simply tired." She wrapped Joseph in a shawl, hoisted him to her shoulder and took Benny's hand, when she saw Vaselik in the doorway, silently watching them depart.

As they left Leah realized that tomorrow the Widow Popov would find a pile of dirty dishes piled in the kitchen, abandoned on the dining table and sitting by the fireplace. She was glad the old shrew would have to clean up the mess that Leah had left behind.

Vaselik was suddenly weary. He poured himself another full glass of brandy and stared into the fire. His military duty required him to sniff out revolution wherever it might occur but tonight only reminded him what a sham it was to celebrate twenty years of disappointments, frustrations, all played out against a background of missteps and lost opportunities.

"How handsome you are my pet." He remembered how proud and playful his mother had been at the ceremonies concluding his first year at the Academy. All the other cadets envied him having such a beautiful mother and kept interrupting them, pretending to need some information from Vaselik, so they would have the opportunity of being introduced to the charming Natasha.

In those days, it seemed then that nothing could deter him. His career stretched before him; he was the star of his class. A royal appointment, the goal of every cadet, seemed assured with the financial support of his family. But then calamity struck and he was just another recruit with no options other than becoming an ordinary officer in the army.

Vaselik stubbed out his cigar, swallowed his drink in one long draught and rued the day he had ever laid eyes on the Widow Peretz.

chapter 17

EVERYDAY, LEAH WENT to the old Rebbe's house to see if any mail had arrived from her family. She couldn't understand why there had been no response to her letter asking for help. She desperately hoped that an answer would come soon.

In the old days, which is how the villagers now referred to the time before the attack, the Rebbe's small place was used as the official post office where the villagers could pick up mail or drop off out-going letters. Then, the Rebbetzin, the Rebbe's wife, earned a little extra money acting as postmistress, sorting the letters and at the same time playing the role of unofficial matchmaker. Eligible boys and girls would use coming to the post office as an excuse to have a chance to congregate together under the pretense of picking up the family's mail. The old woman kept a strict eye on all of them.

Leah had seen the beginning of more than one romance when a boy and girl exchanged whispered hellos and locked eyes. Sometimes they even managed to slip each other a note before the Rebbetzin discovered them. She did not allow any unsupervised contact, her matchmaking had to be conducted under the most strict, chaste circumstances. But Leah was certain that despite the Rebbetzin's restrictions, many romances probably started with that whispered hello right in this very mail room.

Now the eligible prospects had to seek out each other without the Rebbetzin's assistance. She had been so traumatized by the pogrom that she didn't leave her bed for days. The old woman never spoke about what she had witnessed; in fact she barely spoke at all. Today she sat silently, in her big rocker, staring vacantly at the villagers who came into collect their mail. Samuel, the shamus, took over her duties, but he simply handed out the letters. There was no conversation or exchange of village news or help in starting a match like the old woman might have done.

This morning Leah said hello to the Rebbetzin, but didn't expect any reply. The woman remained locked in the world she had created in her mind, one that protected her from memories.

As Leah waited for Samuel to check the letters, a young girl came in, looked around, hoping to see a possible marriage prospect. But the room was almost empty, so the disappointed girl simply picked up her letters and left. All the young men were either rebuilding their wrecked houses or had been forced to leave home searching for work. They had little time for studies or looking for a bride. Ultimately they would turn to the matchmaker to find their *beshert*, their soul mate. Girls with no dowry would be relegated to the bottom of the matchmaker's list and with so many families in dire financial circumstances; there were lots of girls who would not make the list at all. A poor boy could still be considered a catch, especially if he was a Talmudic scholar, but without a dowry, a poor girl had very slim chances to be chosen.

In the past, when there was money, the village Benevolent Society had always tried to help those girls. If Morris hadn't been so anxious to find a wife, Leah might have remained unmarried and still be living at home back in Yanov. Even without a generous dowry, Leah was helped by her father's impeccable learned reputation which satisfied Morris's requirements.

Leah was still concerned at how Vaselik knew so much about the comings and goings at her house. She hadn't seen anyone watching, so who kept him so well informed? He might want her to believe that he cared about her, but his warning simply reinforced her fears that he was just a Russian officer ordered to stop the rebels. She should forget him, but despite her best efforts he stayed in her thoughts. She could still smell the fragrance of oranges that had clung to him that last evening.

Two days later, Yaakov passed through Koritz and came to tell Leah the news about Sarah. "She was stopped by some soldiers and because she did not have papers giving her permission to be out of her home village, she was returned home under the threat of prison."

"Is she alright?" Leah was horrified by the news.

"The soldiers were a little rough on her, but she was mostly scared they would take her off to jail. Females, especially young girls like Sarah, do not fare well in prison."

Leah felt sick thinking about Sarah, alone and vulnerable. Perhaps the girl would not have not been any safer at her house, but Leah felt responsible that she hadn't offered Sarah refuge.

"You also must be careful," she told Yaakov. She spoke very carefully. "The military have been showing a great interest in my family. I'm concerned that they have someone watching the house." She hesitated telling him about what Vaselik said, but she emphasized her warning. "I'm so sorry about Sarah. I'd like to make it up to you if there is anything I can do to help."

"Well, there is one thing," he said, "but if you think they're watching your house, perhaps you shouldn't. A few people here in Koritz were interested in attending our next meeting. It's not a long list, but if you could drop off a leaflet to each of them." He brought out some leaflets out of his satchel.

"Isn't it foolish to have the date and location in print?" she asked.

"Yes," he shrugged. "But there's no other way since we can't always tell them the details in person. Please be extremely careful. I wouldn't ask you if I had any other choice."

After he left, Leah plotted the best way to deliver the material without causing any suspicion. Joseph sat at her feet, cuddling his rag doll, softly crooning baby sounds while Benny recited prayers in the corner, rocking back and forth imitating the old men at shul.

The next morning, Leah proceeded quickly through town, the dirt under her feet packed hard as stone, her breath swirling in the icy air. She wanted to finish this delivery as soon as possible, without drawing any attention to herself. Benny was charged with looking after Joseph at home and she went out carrying a basket, the leaflets hidden underneath a layer of potatoes. To anyone watching, she was just someone wanting to trade potatoes for other foodstuffs. If she were really lucky, perhaps she could slip the leaflets under the doors of the people on her list and not actually see anyone.

First on her list was Eli, apprentice to Simon, the watchmaker. Since neither she nor Morris ever owned a watch, Leah had never met either of them, although she had frequently passed their little shop. It was off the main market area, on a crowded street of tumbledown shops and stalls where shopkeepers or craftsmen rented a tiny area to sell their wares.

Leah cracked open the door, but the bell hanging overhead was missing its clapper and no longer announced anyone's arrival. The place was small, dark and windowless, a jumble of clocks and watches, some of them prematurely chiming the hour. She nodded to the old man hunched over a counter, covered with the mechanisms of dozens of watches, while the clocks on the wall continued to ring out their own version of the correct time.

"Hello. Is Eli here?" It might be cold outside, but the air in the room was sour and stifling, making her so dizzy that she steadied herself against the counter.

"Careful there," the old man cautioned. "Don't disturb the watches." His skin and eyes were yellowed from long hours in an airless room. A few straggly white hairs peeked out from under his kippah, but his beard was full, hiding a thin mouth, an unlit cigarette hanging from one corner. "What do you want with my nephew?" he inquired, his eyes narrowing suspiciously.

"Is he here?" She didn't dare leave the leaflet with someone she didn't know and wasn't sure that the old man would believe her excuse for her visit. Then the backdoor opened and a slight young man of about twenty came in, his skullcap perched atop dark curls which framed his face like the petals of a flower.

"This woman was asking for you," the old man said. "Don't waste a lot of time talking, if she isn't a customer."

"Eli," Leah spoke softly. "Perhaps we could just step outside for a moment. I have a message for you." This delivery business was more complicated than she expected. Once outside, she handed him a leaflet. "This is from Yaakov."

Before he could engage in any further conversation, Leah hurried away, wanting to avoid being seen giving him information. He called out, "Thank you," as she left, but she didn't turn to acknowledge it.

Her heart pounded but she felt exhilarated by her first delivery. This errand might be heart stopping, but the excitement convinced Leah that she was part of a dangerous but important adventure.

The next name on her list was a B. Lavinsky, at the general store, a little further down the street. Leah walked gingerly, careful of the ruts in the road hidden under the snow and mud. She thought about the speaker at the last meeting, how inspiring his words had been.

"These are turbulent times," he had admonished the crowd, "when our country teeters at the edge of an abyss. Russia must reform or plunge into revolution."

She owed it to her children to try and make their homeland a better place. And she also owed Morris to never forget his sacrifice. The faces of strangers she passed suddenly looked sinister and even people she knew, like Gittel who waved to her from across the road felt suspicious. Leah didn't want to stop and talk, but it would look strange if she just rushed by. Anyway, it was too late to bolt, because Gittel was crossing the road and coming towards her.

"Leah, I must thank you," she called out, extending a reddened, chapped hand towards Leah.

"For what?" Leah was caught off-guard by the kind words.

"Yussel. The herbs you gave me cured him. You're as good as Anna was." Despite the cold temperature, Gittel seemed inclined to continue the conversation, her bulky body blocking Leah's way.

"I'm happy he's well," Leah said, relieved by the praise. "But Anna knew what she was doing, I'm just lucky."

She studied Gittel, seeing for the first time, deeply etched lines around the eyes and mouth. Leah wondered if her own face also showed the same effects from recent events and if it was so obvious to everyone. Without a mirror, she didn't get to witness the daily changes. Perhaps it was vanity of a different kind to not look at herself in a looking-glass.

"Where are you off to?" Gittel asked, showing no signs of moving on.

"I have some business to conduct at the store down the way." Being anonymous in Kortiz was not an easy matter.

"Oh, I could come with you if you'd like."

Why did Gittel have a sudden interest in shadowing her? Leah had to get rid of her without making her suspicious. "It would be awkward to have someone else there while I talk business to them. I know you'll understand." With that, Leah veered around Gittel and made her way quickly down the road to the Lavinsky store.

The store was just an area of a room, separated from the family's living space by a curtain of burlap strung on a clothesline. A woman in her forties stood behind the counter, hair covered by a scarf, her face a mask of studied pleasantness, her stiff mouth upturned, as if she had been ordered to smile at people, no matter how she might actually feel. The store was empty of most items still listed on a poster nailed to the wall: flour, candles, matches, salt, needles, cloth. Only a few sacks of grain sat on a shelf.

"What do you need?" she asked sharply. Her tone did not match the forced smile on her face.

"I'm looking for B. Lavinsky." She should have gotten more information from Yaakov about the people on her list.

"What trouble is that girl into now?" The woman sounded annoyed and made no effort at being pleasant.

"None that I know of," said Leah. "Is she here?"

"Becky," the woman shouted. "Get out here."

A very pretty girl, less than twenty, appeared from behind the screen. Her large brown eyes were clear and bright, a sweet smile lighting up her face. "Yes Mama," she said gently.

"Would you mind if I spoke to Becky for a moment?" Leah wasn't sure how to get the girl alone under the prying eyes of the mother, but the girl solved the dilemma herself.

"Come back here," Becky said, pointing to the kitchen table behind the screen, "and have a cup of tea. You must be frozen walking around in shoes like that."

"Remember you have chores to do," her mother warned. "No dawdling over tea and leave the sugar cubes alone."

Leah followed the girl and watched her pour the steaming tea into jars serving as glasses. Becky put her finger over her lips as she took one cube from a tin breaking it in half, putting a piece into each jar.

"She isn't usually so abrupt, it's just things have been so bad lately." The girl's forehead knotted in distress over her mother's rude manner. "But I think I know why you're here," she said in a whisper. "Is it about another meeting?"

"Yes." Leah pulled out a leaflet from her basket and handed it to Becky. "You're so young to be involved."

"Not any younger than some of the most famous women revolutionaries I've read about. Sophie Bardin and Vera Sassulitch were only seventeen and eighteen when they became involved. Girls risked their lives, were arrested, some were sent to jail or even exiled." Becky kept her voice low, but her face lit up when she talked about jail and exile as if they were great triumphs in life, while Leah's heart had started pounding again at the images those words provoked.

"What's going on here?" Mrs. Lavinsky pushed open the burlap curtain, her face puffed out with anger. "Are you the one making my Becky so crazy? You should be ashamed of yourself." The woman raised her hand as if to hit Leah, but Becky grabbed her arm. "She's only sixteen," Becky's mother cried, "and the only child I have left."

Leah apologized for the intrusion, assuring the woman that she meant no harm. As she left, Becky's mother followed her to the street, crying out again, "She's the only child I have left. Leave her alone."

No one paid attention to the woman's ravings, making Leah think that this wasn't the first time Becky's mother had created a scene. But Leah hoped that she wasn't somehow contributing to a disaster for this young and vulnerable girl. These young people, Becky, Eli and Sarah, all amazing, so ready to risk danger. If she hadn't settled into marriage, that might have been her.

"Taking a walk on such a freezing day, Widow Peretz?"

Leah looked up to see Vaselik astride his horse, looking down at her. They hadn't seen each other since his dinner celebration and now she fought against the thrill she felt at his sudden appearance. But she was also relieved that no one she knew could see them in conversation.

"Looking to trade potatoes for other things," she said, making sure that the leaflets stayed safely tucked under the potatoes.

"You don't seem to be having much success, are you?" he said, not unkindly. Without his help, it was obvious that she wasn't managing very well. "Let me take those potatoes in trade for some milk and vegetables."

She pulled back as he reached down to take the basket. "No, I need the basket," she said quickly. "I'll get some paper from the store and wrap up the potatoes for you."

"Don't be silly," he said, tugging the basket from her grasp before she could stop him. "I'll have Sasha pack more food and bring it back this afternoon. Better yet, I'll bring it myself this evening." Nicodemus pawed nervously, his breath snorting out in great bursts of steam. "Until tonight," Vaselik called as he galloped back towards the barracks.

Leah stood stunned, her legs wobbly, fear choking her throat. Vaselik would see those leaflets, he would have her arrested or exiled. She would end up in jail, under the threat of great physical harm. Since the leaflets were face down at the bottom of the basket, under potatoes and burlap, perhaps he would not see them. He might even think it was just paper lining the bottom of the basket. Not seeing them would be a miracle and Leah did not believe in miracles. If only she could take the children and flee, but where? With no money she wouldn't get far.

She was so distraught that she didn't see Samuel the shamus, shuffling as fast as his old legs would take him, waving a letter in his hand. "Leah, your family sent you a letter. I was just coming to give it to you. I know you've been waiting a long time."

A miracle? Maybe there was a God after all. She tore open the envelope, quickly scanned the page, but for a moment she could not believe the words on the page:

Dear Leah,

I am very sad to tell you that Papa died suddenly two weeks ago, may he rest in peace. One minute he was fine and the next, he doubled over in pain, gasping for breath. He was gone before the doctor could even be called. I think the stress of all the recent attacks and his concern about your safety was too much for him.

Dov and I had been thinking about going to America and now with Papa gone, we have made our arrangements. At the end there was very little money, but I have enclosed what we can spare for you and your family. Please talk to Morris about joining us. I'm giving you the address of the friends we are going to stay with.

Love to you, Morris and the boys,

Your brother.

Simon

chapter 18

LEAH STOOD IN the middle of the road, tears staining the letter in her hand. The horror of her situation began to slowly sink in; Papa was dead, Simon and Dov were on their way to America, she was truly alone and desperate. And they hadn't received the letter telling them about Morris' death, so they were unaware of her situation.

The few rubles that were in the envelope would not buy her and the boys train tickets to Hamburg, let alone passage on any of the America-bound ships that left from there, even for steerage. And how could she set out with a young baby on a voyage that she heard could be fatal to the weak and vulnerable crowded in steerage, susceptible to disease, tossed about in a long voyage? Worst of all, at this very minute, Vaselik could be reading the leaflets and planning to ruin her future.

The temperature had been dropping all morning and now flurries of snow began a haphazard journey to the ground, flakes zigzagging in the pale sunlight, bits of crystal floating in the air. Mother nature was laughing at her again, making the countryside so beautiful in the midst of her disaster.

Her life was now tied to Koritz. There would be no refuge at her family's place near the Pripyet River, no haven under the apple tree of her childhood, no shelter in the arms of her father and brothers.

The news of her father's death made her ill and she vomited into a bush by the roadside. Suddenly she was fearful about the boys. She ran home, ignoring slippery patches of snow, sliding and falling, picking herself up quickly. When she reached home, she pushed open the door and yelled for Benny.

He was there at the kitchen table, studying his prayers, but panicked at the terror in her voice.

"I'm here Mama," he cried, his eyes growing wide at her mud-splattered clothes, hair escaping the scarf. He ran to her, thinking she was being pursued, but when no one followed her into the house, he became calmer.

"I didn't mean to scare you, sweetheart. Is Joseph alright?"

Benny nodded yes, but she went in to see for herself that he was indeed okay. She saw that he was sleeping peacefully and came back into the kitchen.

"Uncle Simon sent us a letter with some bad news. Your Zeyda has passed away, may he rest in peace. I don't know if you remember him, but he loved you very much."

Benny had only seen him once when he was very young, but having yet another loss affected him. He kneeled down, putting his head in Leah's lap and she gently stroked his hair. She began humming very softly to him.

"When I was very little," she said, "that was one of my mother's favorite lullabies. And now I can't remember the words."

"My father would swing me up into the air and Mama would always get nervous and protest, 'No David, you'll make her sick.' He laughed and that made me laugh too. Papa's laugh was contagious, when you heard his big booming sound, you couldn't help but laugh with him. He brought me big sheets of paper so I could draw. I'd sit under my favorite tree for hours making pictures of everything I saw. But I especially loved it when he bought me books."

"What about your brothers?" Benny asked. Hearing about Leah's childhood was his favorite pastime. Today it seemed as if his mother was talking to herself.

"They spent a lot of their time studying. I wanted to learn too, but when Mama got sick, it was up to me to take care of her and help run the household. Still any minute I had free, I ran to my books."

It was so ironic that after all the quarrels that she and Morris had over her books, they had all been burned in the attack. Now the only ones she had left were two books of poetry, one from Vaselik.

Leah sat with Benny for a long time, comforted by their physical connection, pondering the seriousness of their circumstances. It grew dark in the room, the wind outside whipping up the falling snow, cold air creeping under the door and through any slight cracks in the walls. Finally she rose, lit a candle and started a roaring fire in the fireplace, not caring that she was using up precious firewood. She stuffed some old rags in the doorway to keep out the cold. After feeding both boys, she bundled them in several layers of clothes under the only heavy quilt and tucked them together into her bed.

She resumed her seat at the table, waiting for whatever unknown fate Vaselik might bring with him. She had to find a way to reach Yaakov as soon as possible before the group's meeting, to warn him about the danger.

Possible scenarios played out in her mind, as the fire died out, embers glowing but no longer giving any warmth. Then she heard a quiet tapping at the door.

"Who is it," she whispered, knowing that it had to be Vaselik, even at this late hour.

"Let me in Leah." Vaselik's voice was low but commanding.

She opened the door, a quick rush of cold air blew in with him. He moved past her, stood in front of the dying fire, his back to her, as if she wasn't really in the room.

"You disappoint me, you really do," he finally said, not turning around.

"I'm sorry you think so." Did he think he owned her, that she would give up her beliefs just because of the attraction between them? "I hope others won't be held accountable for my actions."

"They will have to answer for their own situation. But what am I to do about you?" He turned, his face implacable, not showing anger or pity.

"Surely, Moscow allows people to gather and talk in private homes?"

"Are you mad? These are groups which are fomenting revolt. Do you think the government can ignore all of this? I could arrest you right now and send you off to prison, just on the basis of these printed papers." With that he took out the leaflets from inside his uniform jacket and threw them on the table.

"I cannot go to jail. What would happen to my boys?"

Right now she wanted to kill him as much as she had wanted to harm Morris's killer. To protect her family, she'd do anything. But could she kill the only man who had made her feel alive for the first time in her life? Could she erase the memory of the pleasure that had filled her body?

"You foolish woman, I won't send you to prison, although it will be my duty to stop your senseless activities. And those who directed you must also stop. Otherwise I cannot guarantee what might happen. Do you understand me?"

"And can you understand those of us who are forced to live in misery?" she asked. "You mock Jews who are subjected to constant persecution, but your life has been idyllic by comparison."

"You know nothing about my life," he said. "*Idyllic* is a word that is not even in my vocabulary." Vaselik gripped her arm so tightly that pain shot up to her shoulder. He glared at her intently for a long minute. Suddenly as if a shadow had simply passed over his face changing his mood, his features softened, his lips parted slightly and for a brief moment he looked as if he might lean forward and kiss her. Instead, he closed his eyes, sighed deeply and threw the leaflets onto the hearth, waiting until they caught on fire. Then he wheeled around and walked out.

Leah watched Vaselik leave, realizing that she had been saved from prison, but had truly lost him forever. She went in and lay down beside Benny and Joseph, holding them close, grateful that they would be safe.

chapter 19

VASELIK RODE FAST. Nicademus kicked up mud and snow as they galloped back to the Widow Popov's house. As he got closer, he slowed the horse to a walk, not wanting to arrive just yet. He was angry enough to arrest Leah and all her friends and devastated that she so willingly crossed him, yet through it all he was still smitten, still wanted her. Her face, pale skin, those dark eyes, haunted him. But he was a Russian officer, sworn to the Czar, how could he let her get away with her crime? And, if anyone found out that he had showed her leniency, he could be discharged and dishonored, perhaps even arrested himself.

A figure, panting and breathless, ran out of the shadows, calling him. It was Sasha, his face red, as if the blood under his skin was boiling, his voice hoarse and frightened.

"Captain, come right away. The soldiers have gone mad. They tried to take me prisoner, but I escaped."

For a minute, Vaselik did not move. Mutiny, which had occurred in so many regiments, had finally reached him. He had no idea if he had any supporters in the ranks, except for Sasha, a frightened little mouse who had never looked into the barrel of a gun in his entire military life.

"Please sir." Sasha was nearly crying. "Be careful, they're all armed."

Vaselik wheeled his horse around and rode off to the barracks, Sasha running after him as fast as his short legs could carry him. When the captain arrived at the main door, he dismounted, tied Nicademus to a fence, far away from the building, to keep the animal safe if bullets started flying.

Unsnapping his holster, he took out his gun, holding it casually but firmly in his hand, his arm hanging down by his side, as he walked to the door. It was locked and no one answered his command to open it. He thought about shooting it open, then went to the back door. They had neglected to bolt it and he was about to slip in quietly when he saw Sasha creeping up behind the barracks.

"Wait," Vaselik ordered. "Stay outside until I call you."

In the adjacent storeroom, he waited, listening through the closed door, to the soldiers grumbling in the next room. One complained of back pay owed, another talked about undeserved punishments, while a third sounded nervous about the unrest in the country. Vaselik couldn't tell who was leading the protest. Then he heard Pytor Smirnoff say, "The captain should pay for treating me that way all because of that Jewish slut." So the boy held a grudge for being disciplined and put on half rations. Hatred of Jews and superior officers had managed to bond all the soldiers together.

Vaselik pushed the door open and stood in the entrance, looking slowly at each face. Some of the boys sat on their cots. A few stood stiffly near their beds. No one said a word. The smells of boiled cabbage from dinner still hung in the air. Finally, he said in a measured, even tone. "Who here wants to go before a firing squad as a mutineer? Anybody? How about you Smirnoff?"

Smirnoff turned away defiantly. Vaselik walked slowly through the room, noting who had their pistols strapped to their waists or held them in their hands. They shuffled quietly, taking a step backwards as he strode towards them. When he got closer, the bravado on their faces changed to fear. They look so young, he thought, too young to throw away their lives like this. He lightly nudged Nicholas, a first-year recruit with the tip of his gun, saying "Is it worth dying for a few rubles of back pay?" He leaned over to another, whispering, "Basil, why haven't you come to me if you have a complaint?" Then he stood directly in front of Smirnoff, "You know, Pytor, the leader is always the first to be shot. They'll get you even if you kill me." Smirnoff's ruddy face paled as Vaselik walked to the front of the room. He was acutely aware of every soldier in the place, knowing they all watched his every move, feeling their eyes boring into the back of his head.

If they banded together, they could easily overpower him and take away his gun.

He turned and faced them, sounding very much like a weary father, "Put all your guns away and we'll chalk this all up to a case of group dyspepsia. Continue on and my messenger will reach the authorities with a full report. There is still a chance of stopping him before he gets too far."

The room remained silent for a very long moment. Vaselik wondered if this was how he would die, killed by his own men instead of in glorious battle. He realized that he didn't care if this was his time to go; he was so worn down by his life that perhaps dying was the best answer after all.

Then Nicholas hesitantly put his pistol on the table, a little sheepishly, like an errant boy who had been caught stealing cookies. The others waited, looking at each other for moral support, then one by one, they also laid down their pistols, all except for Smirnoff. Vaselik tried not to act surprised that they acquiesced so quickly. He hadn't expected a mutiny to be so half-hearted.

One of the boys murmured, "What is dyspepsia, anyway?" Smiling at the question, Vaselik answered while keeping his eyes on Smirnoff, who still held his gun, with the hammer cocked.

"A very bad upset stomach." Vaselik told the boy. "You get it if your dinner doesn't agree with you. Maybe you are all suffering from bad cooking."

What is Smirnoff thinking, he wondered. Is he remembering his parents, thinking how beautiful the trees are in summer, budding with white blossoms like virginal girls going to confirmation? Does he wish that he had never started this ruckus, would prefer to be bedding with some girl from the village, enjoying her plump thighs and soft lips? Vaselik's head ached, his fingers grew stiff from holding his gun, when he saw Smirnoff ever so slowly uncock his pistol and place it on the table. The boy turned his back on Vaselik, his last bit of insolence for the night.

"Good," said Vaselik. "I think the drama is finished for now. Sasha," he called. "Come in here."

Sasha stopped for a moment at the door, unsure of what had transpired in the room, but he finally entered, wide-eyed with fear until he saw the pile of guns on the table. "Yes Captain?"

"Collect all the guns, then give these boys a drink of vodka, only one, mind you. After that everyone should get to bed. We're going to have a busy day tomorrow looking for revolutionaries."

chapter 20

LEAH POURED HOT water over the kitchen floor boards and got down on her knees to scrub. It helped to be busy with cleaning chores as she tried to put her thoughts in order. She worried about Yaakov. She had sent him a letter with Anton, the village carriage driver, warning that he must cancel the meeting or at least change the location, but she had received no reply. Anton swore he had delivered it to Yaakov's house, given it to the old man, his grandfather, but Yaakov was not there.

She had a premonition that something terrible had happened and Vaselik was responsible. She was afraid to ask him directly and instead tried worming information out of Sasha. The orderly's face scrunched up, alarming her even more. He looked as if he knew something, but denied everything, his eyes bulging like a fish caught on a hook, then ran off, muttering about an errand he had to do for the Captain.

The monotonous task of scrubbing usually helped to calm her, but not today. As she dipped the brush into the water, she heard a quiet tap at the door. Drying her hands on her apron, Leah opened it to a bedraggled looking Sarah, shivering with cold, in the doorway.

"My god, Sarah, you look ill. Come in child." Leah sat the girl near the fire, massaging her hands to get some circulation going. She removed Sarah's wet shoes, rubbed her feet to warm them and poured a cup of steaming tea from the samovar. "Have you seen Yaakov?" she asked.

"Leah, that's why I'm here," said Sarah. "I need your help. They tried to arrest Yaakov two days ago, in the woods right near Koretz. He had stopped the wagon when he heard rustling in the bushes. He thought it was a buck, his antlers caught in the branches and took his rifle to shoot it when he saw it was soldiers. Somehow he was able to escape into the forest, but they shot after him. He's hurt." Sarah's voice broke, tears streamed down her cheeks as she kept twisting her hands as if that action might somehow summon aid for Yaakov.

The news was like a punch in the stomach to Leah, she could barely take a breath. Finally, she cried out, "Oh my God, it's my fault, all my fault."

It was her worst nightmare. Yaakov had been ambushed near Koritz, an area under Vaselik's command. It must have been Vaselik who ordered the arrest. It was all due to her stupid carelessness. If only she had prevented him from seeing those leaflets. So much of what she and her children enjoyed now was due to the goodness of Yaakov and his grandfather. Their shelter, a dry kitchen, a fire burning in the hearth and in the next room, her boys healthy and warm. If it wasn't for Yaakov, they would still be living in that damp hole of a cellar.

"He's hiding in the woods a few miles from here. If we can't help him, if they find him..." Sarah sounded desperate as her words trailed off. "You know, protesting for reform or revolution could mean a firing squad."

Leah shuddered at those words. Of course she knew the penalties. But now she had to remain calm and think clearly.

"How can we get him back here if he's hurt?"

"When Yaakov escaped," Sarah said, "his horse, scared by the noise of the guns, ran off dragging the wagon behind him. Thank goodness the soldiers didn't go after Drushka too. Some of us worried when Yaakov didn't return and went out looking for him, following his same route. We found him wounded, hiding in the woods and then discovered Drushka a short distance away, waiting as if he expected Yaakov to come for him. I drove the wagon and left it right outside of town. Please, Leah. I came here because I know you can heal people with herbs and poultices."

"Why didn't you bring him here immediately?"

"We were afraid of moving him. And he wasn't sure if you'd want him here, since he's a fugitive."

"Of course he must come here. But we'll have to bring him back when it's dark so we're not seen."

They had to leave right away. There was no choice, Benny would have watch Joseph. "Mama has to go help Yaakov," Leah told him. "He's hurt but I can't take you and Joseph with me. Do not open the door to anyone until I come home. If Joseph cries, rock him and put a little bit of jelly on the cloth for him to suck on. But most important, do not let anyone into the house."

Benny nodded, his face serious as his mother charged him with the protection of his little brother. "Don't worry, Mama," he said.

Leah packed the satchel with herbs and powders, adding some clean cloths and a jug of water. She had become a bit better in her doctoring skills, but still believed that luck played a great part in her treating sprained ankles, a child's cough or bringing down a simple fever, but today she was Yaakov's only chance. There was no doctor in the town and no one else that she could trust to help.

She and Sarah traveled the back roads to avoid being spotted, especially alert if the army was out patrolling. Time had been wasted by not bringing Yaakov to her at once. Now they had to spend extra time locating the wagon and then smuggling him back home. Once Yaakov was rescued and on the mend, she would have to find a way to plead his case.

They passed by fields brightly glistening with snow, preferring to travel through the darker, shadowy woods. As they walked, Leah asked Sarah the same question that she once asked Becky. "You're so young to be taking such great risks."

Sarah spoke eagerly. "The movement has had girls younger than me who were thrown into prison or, like Sonia Peysakhzon and Vera Grabolski, killed during a demonstration. They were the brave ones. I always knew I had to do something to change things for the better." She stopped to catch her breath.

Sarah's answer was the same as Becky's. Their courage put Leah to shame. "But there's so much danger. Look what happened to Yaakov." Leah shuddered, knowing that now she was also a target for this danger.

"When have Jews ever had it easy?" Sarah smiled, looking for just a moment like the young girl she was.

They found the wagon and Drushka patiently waiting for his master. Leah took the reins, although she had never driven before, but the old horse obeyed her readily, going fast at her urging.

It was dark by the time they reached Yaakov. He was semi-conscious, his leg had been wrapped but was still oozing. Leah panicked when she saw him, because his face had the same pasty pallor that Morris had right before he expired. She hoped that she wasn't too late.

Automatically, she offered a fervent prayer. Maybe she was a hypocrite, but she'd take any help, even from the God she'd always disdained. Perhaps tonight, He might pay some attention.

Leah pounded the herbs slippery elm and goldenseal into a fine powder with a pestle, then moistened the mixture with some jug water, forming a thick poultice.

"Yaakov, it's Leah. I'm here with Sarah." He was in too much pain to speak, but his eyes fluttered meaning he understood. Sarah held his head while Leah helped him to drink. She gently cleansed his wound and applied the poultice, binding the wound with strips of fresh clean cloth. The bleeding subsided and she was relieved to see the exit wound where the bullet had gone straight through his thigh. Thank goodness she wouldn't have to remove the bullet, something she had never done before.

Sarah gripped him under the shoulders as Leah lifted his lower body, and with a gentle swinging motion, they hoisted him onto the wagon, covering him almost completely with old burlap sacks, so anyone passing by would assume they were carrying sacks of potatoes. Leah drove Drushka as fast as the horse could go, trying not to jar Yaakov too much. When they reached home, the two women struggled to carry him into the house, as quietly as possible, being careful that no one saw or heard them. Benny came out of the bedroom, but when he saw Yaakov's limp body he began to cry.

"Yaakov is going to rest in my bed for now, Benny. I'll sleep on a quilt on the floor so I can be near in case he needs something during the night. You should sleep up in the loft area tonight."

"No Mama, please. I don't want to be up there alone." He looked terrified at the prospect.

"Alright, sweetheart. You can stay down here next to me." She hugged the boy and kissed the top of his head. "It will be fine, Benny, it won't be like the time with Papa. You'll see, Yaakov will get better." She tried to sound reassuring, but she wasn't convinced herself. "Come, let's make you something to eat. We'll let Yaakov rest for awhile."

Sarah stayed at Yaakov's side, cooling his face with a wet cloth. He became very warm and Leah was concerned that he was running a fever because the wound had become infected. She brewed a tea of hyssop, thyme and licorice root to bring down his temperature and took over while Sarah slept, cleansing the wound and applying a fresh poultice. While she worked she talked softly to him, not sure that he could hear her.

"Please forgive me, Yaakov. It was all such a stupid mistake. It's my fault, but I'll find some way to fix it, no matter what it takes." His eyes stayed closed, but she continued her confession. "Vaselik was angry with me and grabbed the basket with the hidden leaflets before I could stop him. He never said a word so I foolishly hoped he would ignore it, especially after he destroyed the leaflets. It was arrogant of me to think that because he had been kind in the past, that he would give us all the benefit of a doubt."

"I'll go to him," she said. "Beg him to drop the charges against you. I only ask that if anything happens to me, that you keep Benny and Joseph safe." That possibility sent a shiver of terror down her spine. Would she really have the courage to plead on Yaakov's behalf or was she just sounding brave so he would heal faster?

The only person who could help was Vaselik. If he issued the arrest, surely he could rescind the order, tell his superiors that it was a mistake. Pleading for Yaakov would further involve her, but it was a risk she had to take. How could she live with herself if she was the reason that Yaakov went to prison or worse, was executed?

After a sleepless night, Leah decided to state her case with Vaselik that very morning before she lost her nerve. "I'm going to see the captain-in-charge about Yaakov," Leah told Sarah. "Please watch the children until I return. There's some porridge warming on the hearth for all of you."

Before she left, Leah peeked in on the boys who still slept. Benny lay on a blanket next to Joseph's crib. Kissing the tips of her fingers, she gently touched each of them on the forehead, almost as a benediction. Her legs felt weighted with cement, as she walked slowly dreading what lay before her.

At the entrance to the barracks, Sasha spotted her through the open door and hurried out to greet her. "Hello, Missus. If you're looking for the Captain, he's not in his office."

"I'll wait," she said, pushing past the orderly and sitting down next to his desk.

"Oh no," he said, looking red and flustered. "He won't be back at all today."

"Then perhaps you have a pillow," Leah asked, unmoved by his attempt to get rid of her. "Because I intend to wait here, even if I have to stay the night, no matter how long it takes."

"Please, Missus. It will mean my head if you don't leave." He looked as if he might lose his breakfast at any moment.

"Sorry, Sasha. This is more important than even your head."

Leah placed a chair in front of the door to Vaselik's office. She was determined that she would not move an inch. Sasha could call for reinforcements to have her removed, but she'd deal with that if he did. Her insides roiled like she had eaten too much cabbage, but she was committed to helping Yaakov. She imagined him in prison, day after day in a small dark windowless cell, with cold, dank walls, the smells of urine and feces obliterating the air, hearing cries of pain from prisoners in the other cells. Perhaps he, too, would be beaten to get information; all because of her. She didn't want Sasha to see her cry, but she could not erase those awful pictures from her mind.

A shadow crossed her face. Vaselik stood before her, Sasha babbling beside him, assuring his Captain that he tried to get her to leave.

"I was expecting you," he said. "Go into my office."

Leah went in, unsure of what might soften Vaselik's heart. She felt like Moses before the ancient unfeeling Pharaoh. "The boy has done nothing wrong," she began. "Why are you hunting him?"

"You are questioning me? I am doing nothing but my duty."

She saw an open desk drawer, in it a half-empty bottle of vodka. She wondered how many drinks he needed in order to get through his day. Leah had never known anyone who drank heavily, but occasionally a woman in the village shamefully confessed about an unhappy husband who drank too much and took his anger out on a wife or child. These were men who said they believed in God, yet betrayed the tenets of the Torah. What was Vaselik betraying?

"There is duty and then there is doing what is right," she said. "You are lucky; you have the option to make a choice." She looked at him, his face more ruddy than she remembered, maybe from the cold weather, maybe from those swigs of vodka. He still had the ability to make her pulse beat faster, but she would not let his effect on her get in the way.

"You are a silly woman if you believe I can do what I want. I'm under the authority of our Czar. I do what I'm commanded to do." Ignoring her stare, Vaselik reached for the bottle and poured himself half a tumbler of vodka.

"What kind of credit can you reap for yourself by arresting a boy?" she asked. "Someone so far down the list of importance as to be almost invisible."

Despite a cold wind rattling the windows, the sun had reached this side of the barracks and poured into the office. A sun that she was sure Yaakov would never see once he entered his prison cell.

"It's out of my hands now, under the jurisdiction of someone else, someone higher up than me."

"If you're waiting for me to grovel, to beg, look at me." She got down on her knees, touched her forehead to the floor.

"Leah, get up."

He pulled her upright, until they were standing face-to-face. She smelled tobacco on his breath, noticed that he hadn't shaved that morning, perhaps not for several days.

"Please Ivan, try to help him. You may not care any longer for me, but we don't want to be guilty of hurting an innocent boy. I beg you to try." She realized that it was the first time she had ever called him by his given name.

"Do you think I did this out of spite or jealousy of you? Do you think so little of me after all?" He refilled his glass and drained it quickly. He had wanted to hear her say his name so often, but now it was like a knife in his heart.

"You must leave," he said, his face showing no emotion. "I cannot waste any more of my morning on this." He took Leah's arm, pulled her to the door, opened it and gently pushed her out before closing it behind her.

All the tears that she had tried so hard to suppress streamed down her face and when Sasha tried to help, she angrily shook off his hand.

"Don't worry, I'm going," she said.

"No Missus, please, I'm sorry, truly I am." He called after her, but she was already out the door.

Vaselik slumped in his chair, already refilling his glass. He barely felt the burn of the alcohol going down his throat, getting no relief from its heat. He didn't like this feeling of helplessness. Usually after one or two drinks his confidence was restored. Not today. Not after seeing the anguish in Leah's eyes, knowing that she blamed herself and held him responsible for whatever befell this Yaakov. He had been correct in pursuing him, after all the boy was an outlaw, but being correct was not the same as being right. Leah had said it, Vaselik knew it. What could he do to rekindle the look of love in her eyes? What was the right thing to do so he could sleep at night without so much vodka?

"Sasha," he yelled. "Have my horse saddled immediately."

chapter 21

THINGS WERE GOING badly for Vaselik. He had accomplished what he set out to do, to have Yaakov's arrest warrant cancelled, but Vaselik's superiors did not take kindly to the excuse that a mistake had been made.

"Why are you so interested in saving this Jew?" they repeatedly asked him. Telling them he had issued the arrest warrant based on faulty information did not absolve him with those in charge. "Officers are not supposed to make this kind of mistake."

Colonel Novikov and the other officers seemed to be more suspicious of Vaselik than they were about Yaakov. The colonel's cold eyes regarded Vaselik very closely as if he were an insect under a magnifying glass.

The room was stuffy, the proceeding held in a civil building in Kiev, heavy drapes covered the windows, allowing only a little daylight to slip in around the edges. Having to stand at attention during the entire cross-examination made Vaselik's shoulders ache and he felt as if a metal rod had been attached to his spine. In the past Vaselik bragged that he could stand ramrod stiff all day and night if necessary during a dress parade, whether drunk or sober.

The atmosphere today reminded him of visits with his grandfather, when he was made to stand at attention for long periods waiting for the old man to first acknowledge his presence, then what seemed to be forever until he actually spoke to him. This was supposed to train Vaselik at a very young age, in military discipline, according to his grandfather, who had been a notoriously severe cavalry officer in his younger days. Vaselik thought it had merely trained him to hate any authority other than his own.

The colonel huddled with his associates, speaking quietly, while Vaselik pretended to study his nails or the non-existent lint on his uniform jacket, but he noticed that their faces remained stern, without a trace of compassion. He knew how serious the investigation was, but with his exemplary military record, Vaselik thought they might show some humanity, some evidence that they acknowledged his previous loyal service. After a brief fifteen minutes of consultation, Novikov announced their decision. Vaselik had a choice: demotion and transfer to a barracks in an even more remote rural area or resign the military. They gave him a week to decide. Leaving the army under a cloud would cast an irreversible blot on the rest of his life. It would give his grandfather a further reason to berate him and could prevent the old man from releasing any of the funds his mother had left him, a bequest he was supposed to inherit on his 35th birthday, less than a year away. But as the trustee in charge of the moneys, his grandfather could refuse on moral grounds. However, if he accepted the transfer and demotion, it would be a humiliation that would require copious amounts of alcohol to overcome.

He tried to comfort himself knowing he had managed to right a wrong, perhaps even saved a life. The only known facts were that Yaakov and his friends were merely meeting, no other evidence of revolt had surfaced. Unwittingly, Vaselik was mimicking the footsteps of his paternal grandfather, who had been one of the Decemberists, a group of Russian nobles who secretly worked to reform the government, another fact that his maternal grandfather could never forgive.

Perhaps now, Vaselik thought, he had rehabilitated himself in Leah's eyes. At this moment, however, with his life in a shambles, he hated her, and worse yet, despised himself for still hopelessly desiring her. He wished he could erase that chapter of his past, forget her and stop feeling so worthless. Perhaps his grandfather was right and he was a weakling and a drunkard. Certainly his conduct was that of a lovesick schoolboy.

He spent several sleepless, vodka-fueled nights, before deciding to take the transfer. Awake in the middle of the night, with the bottle never far away, he had realized that without the army, his life would descend into endless rounds of vodka, gambling and whoring. Even in the army he might continue those vices, but military discipline would eventually pull him back up.

He informed his superiors of his decision, explained to Sasha that a replacement would be sent to take over command and packed up his belongings. Not much to show for twenty years of service; a few books, a photograph of his mother, his father's pocket watch and the lace handkerchief spotted with red that his mother used to wipe his father's face after he shot himself.

Vaselik was entitled to a few weeks leave, but had no desire to visit family or friends and did not trust himself to be close to the gambling halls of Moscow. Instead, he decided to stay quietly in his rooms until it was time to move on.

***

Sasha knocked timidly on Leah's front door. The last time he saw her was the day she insisted on waiting for the Captain. When she left she was not very happy with either of them and he wasn't sure how she would receive him this morning. After he knocked he heard a lot of shuffling noises inside and then the door opened a crack.

She was about to close the door again, but he held it open.

"Missus, do you think you might come see the Captain before he leaves? I know you were very angry with him and me, too, but really, Missus, I worry about him."

"What are you talking about?" Leah asked. She opened the door a bit wider, having safely hidden Yaakov beneath several quilts on the bed as soon as they heard the knock.

"Well, first of all, I am supposed to inform you that the arrest warrant for the boy Yaakov Dovabovich has been cancelled. I am definitely not permitted to tell you that as a result the Captain has been transferred to a camp close to the Siberian border. And he would have me whipped if he knew that I was asking you to see him before he leaves. I found him yesterday afternoon in his room just staring into space, a pistol on the table in front of him. He hasn't even ridden Nicademus for days. I'm truly scared, Missus."

She was shocked at hearing about Vaselik's transfer, but grateful that Yaakov had been cleared and was a free man.

"Yes, of course I'll come to see him and I promise not to tell anything you've told me." Sasha left grateful for her help.

She would simply go to see Vaselik to thank him for his help, even though the news of his transfer was devastating, Leah was truly grateful to him. She still blamed herself for everything that had transpired, now at least she'd have some peace of mind that Yaakov wouldn't be dragged off to prison.

Before she left for the Widow Popov's, Sarah came to her, looking worried again.

"Is it possible, Leah, that you could shelter another person from the group?" Sarah continued quickly before Leah could say a word. "I was contacted about another girl. Bessie is really desperate. She was jailed once and is not in good shape. She fears being re-arrested and I know she'd never survive, Leah, never."

"What did she do?" Leah asked. Someone was bound to notice her boarding these strangers, causing suspicion in the neighbors. But she felt obligated to say yes. Conditions under the Czar were getting worse all the time, yet there was Yaakov and Sarah still hoping to change things, no matter what they had to endure. She had entered this fight now, even if it was only to provide a place to sleep.

They helped Yaakov up the ladder to the loft, so Bessie could stay in the bedroom.

"Mama, please let me stay up there with him." Benny had become very attached to Yaakov. The boy didn't understand the events happening around him because Leah only told Benny what she thought was absolutely necessary. She repeatedly warned him that he must not talk about their guests to anyone, that she would do the explaining if anyone asked.

"But Mama, is it wrong to give people a place to sleep?"

"No, but some people are angry with them and could do them harm. We have to protect them," she said.

"Like Papa protected us?" His little face grew somber. Whenever he mentioned Morris, his eyes misted and she knew how much he was still haunted by his death.

"But we don't want anyone to get hurt, like Papa did, do we?" She hugged him close, even as he squirmed away to climb up into the hayloft to keep Yaakov company. Besides regarding Yaakov as a great friend, Benny loved the tales that Yaakov related about driving around the countryside. And keeping the boy amused made Yaakov happy.

Bessie was hiding in the woods outside of Koritz until she heard Leah's answer. Sarah went to bring her back to the house. The girl was barely out of her teens, but after beatings in prison, she had trouble walking the distance from her hiding place to the house. She moved with difficulty, leaning on Sarah, shuffling along like a woman of eighty, her arms dark with bruises.

"Thank you, Leah," the girl whispered.

Leah helped her into her own bed and brought a cup of tea, adding two lumps of sugar. Life was getting more and more complicated each day. Making herself useful to the group could become expensive if Leah was expected to feed her guests and dangerous if anyone began to suspect that she was harboring fugitives. And nights sleeping on the floor with Benny curled up next to her did not provide much rest and left her irritated by unimportant details.

After Bessie settled in, she steeled herself for her visit to Vaselik. Before leaving, she checked Joseph, who had been napping in his cradle, but was now awake and happily examining his toes. Seeing his mother, the baby laughed and reached out his arms to be picked up.

"He's a blessing," she thought as she gave him a breast to nurse. "If only we could see the world as new and wonderful like a baby does. To him, even toes are an adventure." She sat quietly for a moment, breathing in his baby milk breath and the odor of lavender which she had sprinkled around his bed, trying to enjoy this rare moment of peace before going to see Vaselik.

As she approached the Widow Popov's house Leah became more apprehensive. She had brought along some freshly baked strudel, a lame peace-offering, but she hoped that Vaselik might be happy to see her no matter what the reason. Taking in a deep breath, she knocked on the door, praying that the Widow was not at home. When the door opened, Vaselik stood before her, unshaven, his uniform jacket unbuttoned, a bottle of vodka in his hand. Leah was startled by his condition, it seemed as if he didn't care who saw him at his lowest.

"Oh, it's you," he said. "I was expecting Sasha." He began to fuss with his buttons and quietly laid the bottle on a table near the door. "To what do I owe this honor?" he asked, his tone razor-sharp.

It was obvious that he hoped to wound her deeply with his words. Despite his tone, he appeared as vulnerable as a child who cannot relinquish a hurt he has endured. She wanted to comfort him, but his aloofness kept her at a distance.

"Sasha told me that you had gotten the arrest warrant for Yaakov revoked and I wanted to thank you."

He looked at her very intently, watching as her cheeks grew warm under his probing eyes.

"My superiors kept asking me why I was so interested in this Jew, Yaakov Dovabovich. Perhaps if I had told them that a woman was involved they might have been more understanding."

"You did the right thing, nothing else." His gaze was like a beam of light shining into her eyes and she instinctively put up a hand up to shield them.

"Did I?" he said. "Maybe I did it because I'm still haunted by your face. Maybe I'll always regret my actions because I can't really explain why I did it. I do wonder why you were so intent on my helping this boy. Is he in love with you? Or perhaps you love him?"

"Don't be silly. If I hadn't been so careless you might never have seen those leaflets. I was desperate and I blame myself for all of this. His problems and now, yours." She reached out to touch his hand. "Please, I'm so sorry for all your trouble. Were your superiors very angry with you?" she asked. His face instantly hardened at her question and she saw how difficult it was for him to accept the military's decision.

"After twenty years of service, including frontline duty, you might think that they could overlook what I referred to as a mistake in judgment, the result of faulty information. However it was not a good day for mistakes. As a soldier I have to accept that."

"What does that mean?" Sasha told her that Vaselik was being transferred but surely that wasn't equal to a court martial.

"A change of scenery with less responsibility," was his curt reply.

"Where will you be going?" He didn't answer. "I will always be indebted to you, Ivan," she said. "And I will miss you." Admitting this was difficult for Leah. "You'll never know just how important you have been to me." She stopped herself from saying any more, afraid she had said too much already. She wondered if the pain she was feeling could be her heart breaking into small pieces.

Tears filled his eyes at the sound of her speaking his name. "Ahh Leah, if only we had met at a different time, in a different place. Such sad words, *if only...*"

He drew her to him, his lips on her hair. His touch still had the power to make her tremble, especially today, knowing that this was their farewell. After a long moment, she made herself pull away. She kissed him on the cheek and turned to leave. It was all so final.

"Be careful, dear Leah," he said. "The next barracks commander may not be so captivated by you and your friends."

With that, he saluted her as she went out the door.

chapter 22

LEAH WALKED HOME slowly, her shoulders slumped, her face tear-streaked. She would never see Vaselik again and they had both acted so casually. It wasn't just romantic nonsense that hearts could be crushed, her chest could barely contain the pain. Why hadn't she had the courage to tell him how she felt, but perhaps it would have done more harm to let him know, now that he was leaving. Their time had been so brief, and yet like Vaselik, she would always wonder what might have been if they had met at another time. She believed in free will, but it seemed that the Fates had intervened with their own, different plan.

Signs of spring had begun to push through the last remnants of winter, but Leah was indifferent to the budding trees, the bright green shoots of grass peeking out and the few brave birds anxious to announce the coming of a new season. Spring might mean new life, but she was still grieving. First Morris, her father and now Ivan.

Leah was so distracted that at first she didn't see Gittel, who stood huddled in her doorway.

"Leah, please what's going on at your place?" She clutched Leah's arm tightly as if she expected her to fly away.

"What do you mean?" Leah had kept Bessie and Sarah out of sight and if anyone saw Yaakov, she hoped they would assume he was staying as a boarder.

"Captain Vaselik is being transferred and God knows who they will send to replace him. This is no time to be doing anything suspicious." Gittel's agitation increased with each word.

"Calm down, Gittel. What specifically are you talking about?" It was imperative to be careful with her answers. Leah wanted to take her neighbor by the shoulders and shake her into realizing that she should also be part of this new revolutionary movement, instead of cowering in doorways, but this was not the time to press Gittel any further. Besides, who was Leah to be preaching to anybody.

"Don't play innocent with me." Gittel pushed closer, wagging her finger in Leah's face. "Strangers coming and going. You're up to something and the rest of us will pay for it."

"You're crazy," Leah countered. "Yaakov is staying in the loft. He hurt his leg and since he's been so kind to us, I'm putting him up."

"How about the two girls? Sneaking in, in the middle of the night. Tell me what's happening. I have a family to protect." Gittel spoke so quickly she doubled over, trying to catch her breath.

"They're two young girls from my old village who have had a lot of trouble in their lives and needed a place to stay. Have you forgotten the Jewish law to help those in distress?"

Seeing Gittel's nervous state, Leah didn't say anymore because she didn't trust Gittel to keep a secret. Vaselik's last words to her had been a warning about the next commander, which left Leah very nervous about Vaselik's replacement. What did Ivan know about him? Even though Yaakov was now free, by hiding the girls Leah was certainly breaking the law.

"I'm sorry Leah." Gittel looked a little chagrined. "I'm just so upset about the Captain leaving. It's strange, it happening so suddenly." She patted Leah's arm, as if to offer an apology.

Inside Sarah immediately greeted Leah with a small pouch. "Bessie meant to give this to you when she arrived, but we both forgot." The pouch held ten rubles. "It's from the Bund, Leah. They'll send something whenever they can. The group appreciates how you've helped us."

That evening Yaakov felt strong enough to join them for dinner. His face had gotten thinner, the skin fitting tightly over his bones, as if he wore a mask that was too small. But he regained his spirits when he heard that the warrant was rescinded, surprised by Vaselik's generosity.

"Why do you think he did it?" he asked Leah.

"I think despite his being on the opposite side, he is a very honorable man." She served the soup, hoping to forestall any further questions.

"You've become one of our heroes, Leah," Yaakov said, toasting her with his glass of tea.

"Our thanks to you," Sarah added, but Leah thought the girl wasn't as enthusiastic about Leah as before and wondered if it had anything to do with Sarah's obvious (at least to Leah) affection towards Yaakov and his being so oblivious.

Benny looked from face to face, not understanding why everyone was praising his mother, but all the compliments made him smile, while Leah reddened with embarrassment.

"Yaakov, I still feel terrible about all that happened to you because of me. Next time I'll be more careful."

Yaakov looked surprised, but pleased. "The next time….?" he trailed off. "Leah, that's wonderful to hear," he said. "Could you do another delivery of flyers and periodicals? I hope to be well enough soon to take over."

He didn't seem to be holding Leah responsible for his arrest which made her feel even worse. By all rights he should be angry.

Sarah interrupted, "You can't jump on and off the wagon yet. Your wound might re-open and become infected again."

There was no doubt that Sarah was concerned about Yaakov's recovery. From the beginning, the girl had never left his side when he was the sickest. But there he sat seemingly unaware of Sarah's interest, his gaze fixed on Leah.

"Drushka and I are a good team," Leah said laughing, even though the prospect unnerved her. Still, she had volunteered and took only a second before raising her glass to say, "I'll do it."

"Oh Mama, can I come with you?" To Benny, the idea of his mother driving a cart sounded like the most wonderful adventure.

"No sweetheart, this isn't a game, it will be hard work." And too risky to involve her children.

"Actually, Leah, it might look better if you had Benny with you," Yaakov suggested. "A child accompanying a woman would raise fewer suspicions."

"Oh please Mama, please," Benny pleaded.

"We'll see," Leah said, determined to keep Benny out of it. "We'll see."

Later after Yaakov had returned to the loft and the children and Bessie were asleep, Leah poured two glasses of tea for herself and Sarah.

"You know Sarah," she said, "I think that Yaakov would make a fine husband for someone, someone just like you, in fact."

Sarah turned red, but didn't say anything.

"I don't mean to pry, but how do you feel about him?" Leah stoked the remains of the fire, waiting for some sort of reply.

"We're comrades, that's all," Sarah said, a bit stiffly. She stood up ready to flee the room, but then she blurted out. "Besides, it's you I think he's most interested in."

"But I think of Yaakov only as a very good friend. My heart is elsewhere." Leah hoped the girl would think she was talking about Morris, even though it was Vaselik's face that she pictured.

"It doesn't matter how you feel, Leah," Sarah said. Her jealously was apparent in her voice. "Yaakov is smitten."

Oh God, she thought, first Vaselik guessed, now Sarah. Am I the only one who has been so blind?

"He's young. He doesn't know what he feels." The last thing Leah wanted was a jealous houseguest; life was complicated enough. "Give him time, Sarah."

chapter 23

AGAINST HER BETTER judgment, Leah allowed Benny to ride with her on the wagon. She agreed to make a delivery to a village just two hours away and she told Benny he could come if he behaved. There was no reason really to emphasize his behavior, since he so rarely ever misbehaved, especially since the attack. It was distressing that she had to constantly warn him to be careful, when she really wanted to encourage him to be more spontaneous again.

She followed Yaakov's explicit directions through the woods, but she was a little nervous and glad to have Benny's company. It was important not to show any fear in front of him, which made her act even braver than she really felt. Benny was convinced that they were embarking on a great adventure and she saw no reason to spoil his fun.

She packed the wagon with a bag of potatoes, some pots and pans and a quilt, so it appeared that she was taking the items to sell in the next town. The flyers and newspapers were strapped to the underside of the wagon. Some of the newspaper articles told about the workers' progress in some areas, but there were also accounts of arrests as well as injuries and killings of protesters, which Leah resolutely put out of her mind as she and Benny climbed up on the wagon. She snapped the whip over Drushka's head and started down the road.

Tall oak trees stood guard on each side of the path, their branches reaching across the road in a flowery kiss. Leah couldn't help feeling a surge of excitement at taking this risk. At last she was participating in something daring. She had the same feeling during her earlier attempts, when her every nerve went taut, her eyes and ears were ultra alert to sight and sound. Sitting there with Benny, she was like a female animal on the prowl.

In contrast, they passed pastoral landscapes, Leon Navarovsky's cow lazily munching a few blades of grass, on the side of the road, enjoying the sun, a few escaping chickens pecking seeds scattered by the trees, an old woman leading her goat tethered with a tattered rope.

Next to her, Benny was engrossed with his carved soldiers. He still jumped at loud, unexpected noises, but this afternoon he happily played games with his toys.

"You know Benny, when I was a little girl, just about your age, my father and I liked to sit in the apple orchard near our house, next to the banks of the river. We would bring our books on a beautiful afternoon like this one and sit there until dinnertime. Of course that was before your grandmother became so sick."

"What did you read, prayer books?"

"No, sweetheart, I loved stories about magic fish or wicked spells, a brave dog who stood guard, or fools who turned into princes. I'll tell you one."

She recounted the tale of Ivanushka, considered a fool by everyone, especially his two clever brothers.

"But Ivanushka was the good son who kept watch over his father's field while his two brothers fell asleep and did not see who trampled the wheat during the night." Leah looked down at Benny paying rapt attention. Why had she never taken the time before to sit and tell him stories?

"He discovered that it was a magic stallion, Silva-Burka," she continued, "wearing a gold saddle and a silver bridle who had been destroying the fields. Ivanushka managed to catch the horse by the collar the next night and in exchange for letting him go, the animal promised to help Ivanushka anytime he needed it. He just had to call the horse's name, Silva-Burka."

Drushka kept stopping to nibble grass and needed frequent prompting to keep him on the path.

"Go on, Mama, finish the story."

"Well, the Czar, who had no sons, wanted to find an heir, so he announced a contest where he placed his beautiful daughter on top of a tall tower and said that anyone who could jump on a horse and grab the ring from her finger, would win her hand and become a prince and the Czar's heir. Many people tried, but no one could do it, including the two clever brothers. Then Ivanushka secretly called out 'Silva-Burka,' and the horse appeared. The boy climbed into the right ear of the horse, came out of the left one, but now he had changed into a handsome, well-dressed young man. Riding on the back of the horse, he managed to grab the princess's ring and rode off quickly, before turning back into his usual self, but with his hand bandaged."

"How could he go into the horse's ear? Look at Drushka's ear, I couldn't fit into that, could I?" Benny laughed at the thought of such an extraordinary spell.

"No sweetheart, I don't think anyone could, but with the help of magic, Ivanushka did. Later that night, the Czar gave a big banquet, where he invited everyone in the village. His daughter noticed Ivanushka's bandage and asked him to take it off. When it was removed, guess what she saw?"

Benny shook his head.

"She saw that he wore her ring. Ivanushka quietly whispered Silva-Burka's name one more time and the horse turned him into that handsome man again and the Czar gave Ivanushka the hand of the princess in marriage and named him his heir.

"Did you like the story?" Benny shook his head yes. "Besides magic," Leah asked, "what do you think the story is about?"

Benny thought for a minute. "If you have a good friend to help, you can win."

"Yes, that too," Leah said. "But, also, sometimes we judge people too quickly, we decide that they're slow or stupid without giving them a chance."

"Yes," said Benny, "but Ivanushka needed his magic horse. If Papa had had a magic horse, they wouldn't have killed him." His dark eyes grew even darker, his little face pinched with sad memories.

"Sometimes, even magic can't help, Benny." Leah reached out and gently stroked his cheek.

"But why did those soldiers want to hurt us? Sasha is a soldier and he's good to us." He bit his lip so hard to keep from crying that it began to bleed. Leah wrapped her arm around him, drawing him close.

"When people are scared and angry they can do evil and stupid things, like the people who attacked our village, hurt Papa and our neighbors. Some people don't like Jews and believe lies that they hear about us. Other people like Sasha [and she thought Vaselik, but didn't say his name] stay good and kind, even when things are bad all around them. Look how Yaakov and his grandfather helped us. And we tried to help Mrs. Wolf and Sarah."

When they had arrived at the village, all conversation stopped. Leah drove the wagon to the house that Yaakov had described. It resembled most of the houses, with its wooden entry door and a thatched roof, but hanging at the windows were brightly colored yellow curtains just as he said. A young man came outside and led Drushka to the back of the house. She told Benny to go inside the house to get some water and then she instructed the young man, who introduced himself as Isaac, where the hidden packets were. The delivery was completed in a matter of minutes.

Isaac offered Leah and Benny some food, but she declined, saying, "I think it's best if we start back home before it gets dark."

"Then, please," Isaac said, putting some apples into a bag, "take a jar of tea and some fruit for you and the boy."

They settled back up on the wagon, Benny already munching one of the apples, and started home. Leah's breasts had begun to hurt and she was anxious to return and nurse Joseph. Drushka kept slowing down and it took all her ingenuity to keep him moving. She stopped to give him water and let Benny eat a snack of cold potatoes and tea, but they did not linger too long. It was exhilarating that everything had gone so smoothly but she didn't want to tempt fate by being out on the road after dark.

By the time they reached home, Benny had fallen asleep, his head in her lap while her breasts felt as if they could explode. Leah hurried into the house carrying the boy and found Joseph on the bed with Bessie playing number games with his fingers and toes. Leah took the baby to nurse, which gave her breasts some relief. Even though she knew that she should start weaning him, she so relished their connection, that she couldn't bear to break that bond.

After everyone was in bed, Leah sat in the kitchen reveling at the amazing day she had had. Neither Morris nor Vaselik would have ever appreciated her excitement at being involved in this adventure, part of such an important cause. She could hardly wait for the next opportunity, telling herself that she did it for the future of her boys, but knowing that really, it was for herself as well. Her heart had pounded during the ride to Vastov, but she had successfully completed the task. She had truly joined the revolutionaries.

chapter 24

TRUE TO HER promise, Leah agreed to do more deliveries. She took flyers, newspapers, and sometimes money to groups in nearby villages. Benny was restricted to only occasional rides with her because school had finally started again at the Rebbe's house. One of the older Yeshiva students replaced the Rebbe in educating the younger boys. The Rebbe was still quite frail, wandering about Koritz, stopping strangers to ask the whereabouts of his wife and shamus, forgetting that they both were at home. The daily routine of going to school helped Benny regain some sort of normalcy and quiet his fears.

From the beginning, she had let him recite Kaddish for Morris, even though he had not been bar mitzvahed yet and Jewish law did not consider him old enough to participate in certain prayers. But reciting prayers for the dead strengthened his connection to his father and helped him with his mourning. Sons were expected to perform that ritual for their parents and she knew she made the right decision after Benny confessed how guilty he felt that his father died protecting him. By reciting the Kaddish Benny felt he was fulfilling his duty to his father.

"Benny," she told him, comforting him, "Papa saved us all. But you were his eldest and he wouldn't have been able to bear it if you had been hurt."

This morning she drove off alone to deliver news about a rally that would be held in Kiev. It was a glorious spring day, liquid sunshine warming the countryside. Given a little time, even the most barren tree would soon be enveloped by blossoms.

Bessie and Sarah still boarded with her, looking after Joseph when Leah was out on a delivery. The girls treated Benny and Joseph like their own little brothers, telling stories, playing games, singing songs. Even though she was only a few years older than they were, Leah felt almost maternal as if they were the daughters she had lost. Time could not erase the pain of the deaths of Rachel and the two other still born babies. The sadness never really went away.

Leah and Drushka were old friends by now and the horse needed very little prodding to keep on route through the woods. He knew that he would get his favorite treat, apples, if he responded well to her commands. For the first time since childhood, Leah had the luxury of time to think and day-dream as she went out on these trips. The daily struggle of scavenging for food was eased by occasional funds the Bund provided.

Riding along, she cataloged the ten years of her marriage, clinging to the hope that Morris had found some happiness before he died. She had given him two sons, the dream of every Jewish male. And to please him, the family strictly followed Jewish observances, even the ones Leah complained about, those that limited female participation. But there were all the times they argued, especially over finances. How cruel for Morris to be struck down on the very day he was to start work at the mill. He never expressed what he was feeling, always so stoic. That always made her crazy.

She also thought of Vasilik, despite attempts not to. How could this affair, forbidden by everything that she had been taught, be the most ex-hilarating time of her life? To feel a closeness, however brief, to be in the thrall of something she couldn't control or deny had been both wonderful and frightening.

What now amazed her was how similar was the excitement she felt in the midst of danger. She wondered about those young revolutionary hero-ines, the ones who inspired Becky and Sarah, when they had taken risks, what did they feel? To Leah, it was like standing at the edge of a precipice and trying not to fall. You stand poised, but don't know the outcome.

If she hadn't been so engrossed in her thoughts she might have heard the rustling of leaves behind her, the bushes moving without a breeze to stir them. She might have heard the footsteps quietly creeping close. Suddenly the wagon was surrounded by four soldiers, their weapons pointed at her.

The image of Yaakov being ambushed flashed across her mind, she also remembered how Bessie had been arrested and hoped that she wouldn't faint in fear.

One of the soldiers demanded, "Where are your papers?"

She reached into her pocket, but a second soldier knocked her hand away with his rifle.

"I am just getting my identification," she said, forcing her voice to sound calm, even though her heart pounded so loudly she was sure the men heard it.

"Just making sure there are no tricks." he said. "I'm watching."

"Ahh, it's the Widow Peretz," he said, checking her papers.

The other two started poking in the wagon, overturning the bag of potatoes, lifting the pots and pans with the end of their guns. Her mouth turned very dry, like a dusty road at high noon, but she didn't move or protest. When they did not find anything, she expected them to wave her on. Why did they stop her in the first place?

"Come down off the wagon," demanded the first soldier, taking charge, his manner so confident. Too confident for his young years, she thought. His blonde hair shone in the spring sun and he looked like a child playing soldier.

Leah climbed down, not happy at being on the same level as the men. This made her feel too vulnerable. Now that they finished searching the wagon they turned their attention to her. She stayed in front of the wagon, wanting to jump back up as soon as she had the chance.

"Weren't you the old Captain's cook?" asked one of the boys. He also had a cocky air, no doubt boosted by the gun he held so casually in his hands. He smiled, the kind of sweet smile a young boy might flash when he was hiding some mischief. "I miss your cooking. The cook now burns everything." She smiled back, hoping to seem friendly.

"Ivan Vaselik wasn't so old, Nicholas," said the first one. "But I did hear that this Jewess cooked for him at his rooms, didn't you?" He leaned close to Leah, his mouth twisted into a nasty smirk. "What kind of food did you make, Jewess?" He emphasized the last syllable, drawing out the *ess* sound, until he almost whistled it.

"After the attack, I was hired to cook for the barracks but only for a short while," Leah said. "I was let go because your comrades wanted to make their own meals."

"Ahh, the attack," Nicholas interrupted. "Some of us were punished for participating. But that was a lie that the villagers told. Were you one of the people who complained?" He turned to one of the others. "Was she, Pytor?"

There were no friendly smiles now. She saw a coldness that could have only resulted from years of simmering hatred. She knew that her being a woman would not matter to them, remembering the bloody deaths of Mrs. Rodinsky and Anna Vashenko. Soldiers who came from the peasant class often grew up believing that Jews were their enemy.

"Why are you traveling alone through the woods? I thought Jewish women were kept at home," asked the one called Pytor.

The youngest looking soldier moved closer. He seemed the most nervous to Leah. He kept toying with the catch on his rifle, reminding her of Benny playing with his toys. Thank God she hadn't brought Benny with her today.

"I'm a widow and I need to sell some things to feed my children." She hoped that her plight might stir some forgotten strand of pity. But their faces showed no signs of compassion.

"Perhaps she's a revolutionary spy," Nicholas said, using his gun to rifle the edge of her skirt, lifting it up a few inches. "She could be carrying a weapon under all that material."

"No, I assure you, I'm just a poor widow, the only support of my two boys. Please let me go on my way."

Rivulets of sweat trickled down her back and the metallic taste of bile filled her throat. She started to make a move toward the wagon, but Nicholas pushed her so hard and so fast, that she lost her footing and fell onto the ground.

The four soldiers stood over her, two of them pinning her arms with their rifles. They peered down as she looked up at their faces, horrified by the same look of contempt in all of their eyes. Pytor straddled her, beginning to fumble with the buttons on his pants. She closed her eyes and wondered if she would ever see her boys again, when a voice sounded behind them.

"What the hell are you doing?"

All the men turned to see another soldier come into the clearing. She couldn't see his face at first, then saw that it was the boy who had killed Morris. She felt all hope was lost now. He would have the chance to finish the job he started that awful night. He pushed his way through the other soldiers and when he saw her, his face whitened.

"Let her up. **Now**," he said. His tone had such command that the others hesitated only a moment before stepping back so Leah could stand up.

"What's it to you anyway, Viktor?" Nicholas asked. "We were only having a bit of fun." His mouth drooped sullenly, his cheeks reddened.

"I'm in charge of this patrol," said Viktor. "I give the orders."

Morris's killer looked straight at Leah. He gave no indication that he recognized her and she averted her eyes, too afraid to breathe until she was safely up on the wagon. She did not trust this sudden display of kindness. Perhaps he was just playing a sadistic game of cat and mouse and she was the offending mouse.

"Go home, woman," Viktor instructed. "It's not safe out here in the woods. Too many rogues."

She scrambled up on the seat and roughly yelled to Drushka to go, then cracked the whip on his back to reinforce her commands. The startled horse, so unused to the lash, galloped away quickly. After traveling some distance, but afraid to stop, she leaned over the side and heaved until her stomach was quite empty.

chapter 25

LEAH REACHED HOME, trembling and nauseated, her stomach quite empty was still heaving. She managed to get inside before nearly collapsing in the kitchen. Sarah came running out of the bedroom area, gasping at Leah's appearance.

"What happened?" Sarah cried, helping her to a chair. She looked around for a wet cloth to cool Leah's face.

"Four soldiers came out of the woods, pointed their guns at me and...." Leah sobbed and could not continue.

"Did they hurt you?" Sarah asked.

Bessie hobbled into the kitchen, alarmed at seeing Leah's distress. "Leave her alone. Give her a chance to catch her breath."

"It's alright," Leah managed to say. "The soldier who killed my husband came looking for the others and saved me. I don't know why. Maybe a guilty conscience."

"They have no conscience," Bessie said. She looked as upset at the account as Leah. "But you're safe now." She stroked Leah's hand, unable to hold back her own tears. "It could have been real bad. I know."

"She's not that safe," Sarah countered. "None of us are. You can't take any more chances doing deliveries." She poured a glass of tea from the samovar for Leah, her own hands shaking as she set it down on the table. "None of us are safe." Sarah sounded angry as if she held Leah responsible for the soldiers' actions.

Leah slowly sipped the tea, trying to speak calmly. "I'm afraid for my children. They knew who I was. It was almost as if they were waiting for me."

"We have to tell Yaakov and let the Bund leaders know," said Sarah. "There might be someone who is spying on us."

"No one in this house can do anything risky." Leah spoke firmly. "My children could be in danger. If you stay here you must promise to do nothing."

She kept seeing the soldiers, the four pairs of eyes leering down at her, as if they were able to see through her clothing as she lay there completely helpless. She was filled with an overwhelming rage. If only she had a gun, she would gladly kill them. She would hunt them, force them to lay there as defenseless as she had been.

"Joseph, is he alright?" She didn't wait for an answer but rushed in, relieved to find him napping peacefully. He lay on his back, one hand clutching the rag doll that Yaakov had made for him. She sat down on the floor next to his cot and wept. What if that boy had not appeared when he did? Why did he intervene? How did the soldiers happen to be there? Who could want to see her hurt?

That night Leah kept Benny close to her as she stayed awake, sitting propped against Joseph's bed. Both boys had to stay in sight while she remained on guard. If the soldiers knew who she was, they must know where she lived. Bessie offered to sleep on the floor so Leah could get some rest in her own bed, but Leah refused, insisting that she wanted to be alert in case of trouble. She thought back to the night of the attack and how Morris made them hide in the cellar. This time she was the one in charge. They couldn't return to the cellar because Benny was too easily disturbed by any change in routine. To keep him from becoming alarmed, she pretended that nothing was wrong. When they both were asleep, she was finally reassured by their steady, rhythmic breathing.

The next morning she dressed still distraught by the events of the previous day. One thought kept reoccurring which she tried to push aside. Since Gittel had been so upset at seeing strangers at Leah's house, could she have gone to the authorities? It would be devastating to believe that a friend would turn against another Jew and for what price? What sort of reward or favor would be bestowed on an informant? The idea that Gittel might have betrayed her was like a worm boring its way slowly into Leah's brain, a snail leaving behind a trail of suspicion. The only way to know was to confront her neighbor.

Sarah tried to talk her out of speaking to Gittel. "Don't make any unnecessary trouble," Sarah said. "If she did it, we won't give her any future cause for concern. If she didn't, you'd be foolish to create any hostility."

Bessie was particularly fearful that Leah would confront anyone. "Please, I'm so afraid of being taken back to prison. I can't go back."

Sarah took Leah aside and confided that two guards had assaulted Bessie when she was jailed, leaving her both physically and emotionally wounded. She made Leah promise not to reveal that she knew what Bessie had endured.

But Leah was not convinced that talking to Gittel could make things any worse. After the ten years that she and Gittel had been neighbors, Leah didn't want to believe it, but the possibility was there. The woman had been agitated merely by the presence of strangers at Leah's house. What would she do if she suspected that Leah was involved in illegal activities? A hint or two in the right ear? A way to gain favor with the new commander? Since Vaselik's departure, Leah had not spoken with Sasha, but he might know. She'd ask him and then decide what to do about Gittel.

Just approaching the army camp made Leah uneasy, her hands were icy, her stomach turned upside down. It would be unbearable to cross paths with any of the soldiers who had threatened her. She had hidden a kitchen knife inside the shawl that was wrapped around her shoulders, which at least gave her an illusion of protection.

It suddenly occurred to her that Sasha might have been transferred or was no longer working as orderly to the captain-in-charge. Opening the door, she was relieved to see his gnome-like figure hunched over his desk. She almost expected Vaselik to stride out of his office full of confidence and swagger, but the door to the captain's office remained shut.

"Sasha," she whispered.

He turned around, his face lighting up with a smile. "Missus," he said. "I hope you've been well."

"Until yesterday." she said. "Yesterday afternoon I was stopped by four of your soldiers in the woods and threatened, almost attacked." Her words stumbled out, each one whispered with so much difficulty that a nervous tic begin to twitch in her left eye.

"Oh my God, Missus, I am so sorry. Did they hurt you?"

"They would have, but another soldier arrived and ordered them to stop." The tic worsened as she talked and she angled her body slightly so Sasha would not see it.

He pretended not to notice, shuffling some papers on his desk. "Did you come to make a complaint?" he asked.

"I don't know if that's wise, yet. But please tell me if you know anything about it," she asked. "Did anyone from the town complain about me to the new captain?" She saw him hesitate and worried that coming here was not a good idea. Why should the orderly jeopardize his job and help her?

"Captain Koskov is very strict officer, he proceeds exactly according to regulations. He would have issued some sort of order if he wanted the soldiers to apprehend you. I've seen nothing nor heard anything about that."

Was he telling the truth? She couldn't be sure, even though she hoped he was. Before she left, there was one question that she had to ask.

"Have you heard from Captain Vaselik? Is he doing well?"

Sasha grimaced. "He's Lieutenant Vaselik now. He wrote that he's well, but I have a friend who's stationed at his camp. My friend said he's not so good, barely doing as well as can be expected out there in the wasteland. I wanted to go with him, but he said the conditions would be too severe for me. I don't think he wanted me to see him in his demoted predicament." Sasha's voice cracked as he spoke, his face becoming reddened by emotion.

"I'm so sorry to hear that." The news was heartbreaking, made even worse seeing Sasha's distress. She took his hand. "Thank you Sasha. Be well."

"Missus, wait a moment. Take these for the boy. I know he likes sweets." He opened a desk drawer, pulling out a bag of sugared walnuts which he handed to Leah. "I miss seeing him."

Walking back home, Leah decided that she would accomplish nothing by confronting Gittel, even if she didn't agree with Sarah and Bessie's argument about not stirring up muddy waters. She no longer trusted her neighbor, but at the same time, she understood Gittel's fears. Leah had to work hard not to give in to her own fears, not to let them eat into her soul and make her turn against friends. She wanted revenge, but for her, it would be best achieved by an act of protest. Continuing her rebellion would help to free her from the memory of those soldiers taunting her, making her afraid. She needed to show her children that the best way to stay strong is not letting your fears win.

Entering the house, Leah heard Sarah and Bessie whispering with Yaakov up in the loft. She climbed up, peering over the ladder to see if something new had happened. "Is everything alright?" she asked, offering each of them some of the sugared walnuts that Sasha had given her.

Benny was at still at school; Joseph lay on a blanket next to the girls, happily playing with a homemade rattle, giggling every time he heard the tiny bell which was sewn inside.

"The girls told me about yesterday," Yaakov said. He looked pale and drawn, his thigh was not healing as quickly as they had expected. He winced in pain as he sat up. "It's not safe for the girls or you if they remain here. I'm going to take them to another member's place in either Vastov or Umann. I was even thinking about going to Kiev. In a big city they'd be more anonymous."

"Yaakov, you're not fit yet," said Leah. "And just so you know, I am not going to confront Gittel. Not for the reasons you two gave me," she said looking at Bessie and Sarah. "But it's useless to expect her to admit anything and if she did, I'd be so angry I might do something foolish. But I refuse to let fear infect me, like some sort of contagion. I'll take the girls, but Kiev is out of the question. I can't leave the children for that long."

"If we got to Umann, someone else could take us further, if necessary," Sarah said. "But Leah, it's risky for you to be involved."

"You two will have to be hidden. I think that if anyone is actually watching, it might be less suspicious if I continue to pretend to be selling things in other towns. If I stop, I look guilty. Besides, the soldiers never found anything illegal on the cart."

Yaakov protested, worrying about the danger, but eventually Leah wore him down with her confidence. She was sure that her plan would succeed, but it was nescessary to move Bessie and Sarah out as soon as possible.

After arguing, Yaakov finally admitted that he did feel too weak to make the journey and promised to take good care of Joseph and Benny.

The next morning, before first light, the girls got onto the wagon, hiding under a layer of blankets, with bags of pots and pans and various vegetables laid over them. They wanted to leave before sun-up so there would be less chance that anyone would see them. Leah brought along some bread, apples and tea for the journey, feeling a little less confident in the morning than she had been last night. She was glad that they were departing immediately so there wasn't any time for her to reconsider. The directions Yaakov gave her took her away from the woods, suggesting instead the main roads which he thought would be safer than the forest with its many hiding places.

"If it's dark when you arrive," he instructed her, "spend the night at the house. It's too risky to travel at night. Please don't take any chances."

Leah left food warming on the hearth for Yaakov and the children and the girls helped him downstairs. She tried not to frighten Benny, explaining to him how important it was to take Sarah and Bessie home.

"But Mama, I'll miss them. I thought maybe they would stay with us here forever."

"No sweetheart, they can't do that. Please be good and help Yaakov with the baby." She hugged him tight until he wriggled away.

"I can't breathe," he said laughing.

It was time to go. The first rays of the sun would soon begin to paint swashes of color across the sky and turn the clouds into vast pink confection.

Drushka moved more slowly pulling the extra weight of the girls, but he quickened his pace every time Leah snapped the whip above his ear. She couldn't bear to lash him but she saw that the noise startled him into a faster trot. They soon left Koritz behind, but it was many miles before Leah relaxed enough so she didn't see guns pointed at her at every turn. Fields stretched out on either side of the road, sheaves of wheat golden in the sun, the scene a peaceful landscape like paintings she had seen in books by Monet or Van Gogh.

Sarah tented the edge of the blanket so she and Bessie could breathe fresh air and every so often she peered out at the passing scenery.

"It will look suspicious if anyone sees a pair of eyes peeking out from under the blanket," Leah cautioned. "Are you both alright under there?"

"We're a bit cramped, but fine," Sarah answered.

"A little later I'll look for a spot that is off the main path," Leah said, "so you and Bessie can stretch your legs and keep the circulation going. But we mustn't linger too long."

They passed other carts whose drivers seemed surprised to see a woman driving alone. She nodded to them, acting as if being alone was the most natural thing, while her heart pounded loudly. Being out in the open made it less likely that soldiers could sneak up and ambush them, but if she were stopped, there was no way for Leah to outrun any pursuers or give a plausible explanation as to why two girls were hidden under layers of blankets.

Several hours later, they arrived at the new place, greeted by the couple whose house had become a way station for those in need of safety. It was hard saying goodbye to the two girls, more like leaving family as Leah drove off waving a teary farewell. Like Benny, Leah would miss their company. She so admired Sarah and Bessie, who refused to be limited by their gender. They might be young, but they were brave in the face of danger. Even Bessie, didn't allow her own hurt stop her from continuing the cause.

The trip back was tiring and Leah's breasts were full of milk and painful. It was time to start weaning Joseph from the breast. He was old enough even if she was loath to give up that special connection.

By the time twilight's soft silvery light enveloped the countryside Leah decided that it would be quicker to take a short cut through the woods for the last couple of miles so she could get home sooner. She weighed the possibilities and decided that getting home faster would make up for any nervousness she might feel in riding in the woods. Without the extra weight of the girls Drushka was able to keep up a good pace.

Her mission successfully completed, Leah relaxed enough to re-read the most recent letter she had received from her brothers, now settled on New York's Lower East Side. Dov was delivering milk in the neighborhood and Simon had learned to cut patterns for making women's clothes. They shared a room in a family's apartment and insisted that she and the children should join them now that Morris was gone. Leah and the boys would stay with them until she found a job and a room of her own. But how could she make the trip without enough funds? Since today was her last delivery, there would be no more money coming from the Bund. She needed immediate employment, and prayed that the job at Holstein's mill would be available soon.

There was a faint sound of hoofs as she rode home, like an echo of Drushka's steps. For protection, she reached down under the seat and checked that a heavy wooden cane was still there. No one would ever threaten her again without suffering some blows themselves. She pressed Drushka to move faster.

Then she heard a voice say, "Please don't be frightened. I just wanted to be sure you kept safe."

Wheeling around on her seat, she saw that it was Viktor, the soldier who had killed Morris, the one who had saved her life. He guided his horse next to the wagon, appearing to be out riding alone. He seemed different today, anxious, uneasy at their meeting. The night of the attack he had been overly confident, a soldier ready for battle, the other day, a commanding presence. As he rode closer, she thought his uniform looked sizes too big for him.

"You've been following me," Leah asked. "Why?"

"It's as I said, I wanted to make sure you stayed safe. I saw you enter the woods, not a very wise thing to do, especially after what happened." His horse snorted, ready to be on its way.

"You confuse me," she said. "You protected me once, but you're also the one who killed my husband. What kind of devilment are you playing?" Talking this way might be very reckless, but she was compelled to understand who this young man was and what he was doing.

"The night of the attack on the village keeps haunting me," he said. "I've killed in battle before and had no problems afterwards, but that time was different." His voice dropped to a whisper as if he didn't want the trees of the forest to hear his confession. "I have these dreams."

But his words actually scared Leah even more. This might be a trick to get her to lower her guard so he could hurt her in some new way. Or perhaps he saw her as an impediment to his comfort and he decided to rid himself of her. Why was he sitting there looking unhappy?

"I can see your husband protecting his boy and you," he said, "so frightened, yet being brave. I dream this every night and then see it everyday. Sometimes I think I'm out of my mind. Please, I'm so sorry."

He made no sense to her. The soldiers all killed with no conscience, yet he kept insisting that he was sorry. The afternoon grew darker, she was entirely alone, this all could be a trick. He stayed frozen on his horse, looking transfixed at some far-off spot. Her path of escape was blocked by his horse, who kept pawing the ground. Suddenly Viktor leaned forward, abruptly reaching towards her. Was he going to seize her and finally kill her? That would free him of his torment.

Leah panicked. She reached under the seat and quickly grabbed the hidden cane. She came up swinging. She swatted his hand away, to make him leave her alone, but when she swung, all the fury of the past weeks burst inside her: the horror of Morris's murder, the destruction of the village, the humiliation of the attack by the soldiers, the taunts at the barracks raged up inside her. She swung with such force that he was knocked off balance. His horse reared and the boy fell backwards, hitting his head against a large rock.

He lay there, his eyes open, not moving, not making a sound. His horse nuzzled his body as if to wake him up. Leah felt paralyzed, her arms and legs were useless, she couldn't move. She forced herself to slide off her seat. She had to check if he was still alive. There was very little blood, just a little trickling out underneath his head. She leaned closer to test his breathing, but felt nothing. She put her ear next to his chest, but heard no sound of a beating heart. She had become an expert in the realm of death, knowing when the once living had either survived or succumbed.

But this was an accident, she hadn't meant to kill him. She convinced herself that she just wanted to keep him at a distance. Without Vaselik, who in authority would believe that she was innocent?

There was no one she could tell, no one who would believe her. Confessing, even if it was an accident, would trap her in a web of circumstances that she could never escape. She had to leave him. Leah got back on the wagon and drove home. When they found him, they would see he died after an accidental fall off his horse. No one would suspect anything else. There would be nothing to connect her to the accident. If she were arrested, it would not bring him back and what would happen to her children? She wished she could forget the voice in her head, the sound of his last words, "I'm sorry."

"I'm sorry, too," she whispered. But was she? Perhaps after all, this was simply justice. Leaving the wagon behind the house, unhitched the horse and gave him a pile of hay, moving as if she were in a trance. Inside, she heard Yaakov and Benny laughing in the bedroom, but she made no effort to join them. She sat down by the hearth, the energy drained from her body, feeling she was in some icy hell, where all she kept hearing were the words, "I'm sorry."

It was dark in the kitchen, candle light drifted from the bedroom, as Yaakov pulled back the curtain and limped out, leaning on Benny.

"We thought we heard you come in," he said. Seeing the pained look on her face, he sent Benny back to the bedroom. "What is it, Leah?"

"I have to leave Koritz," she finally said. "Take my children and join my brothers as soon as possible." As she spoke a slight tremor began under her left eye.

"Did something happen?" Yaakov asked. He pressed cautiously because Leah looked as if the slightest pressure might break her into little pieces, jagged bits that would never again fit together.

She just repeated that she had to take the children to America. After a silence she said, "Perhaps Mr. Holstein is ready at last to give me work. I have very little to sell but I do have two family pieces that I buried the night of the attack. I'll sell them. Whatever I have to do."

"Do you want to tell me what happened?" he asked.

"I'll write my brothers," Leah continued. "They will have to send some more money."

"Did something happen to the girls?"

"No, they're fine," she said. "It all went according to schedule. I've just had time to think. Leaving is the best plan."

"Do you think it is so easy in America? I've heard from others. It's crowded, dirty, people are poor, no gold on the streets." He looked distressed by her decision to leave.

"But people live free, not afraid. They're not killed in the night or threatened in the day."

"Stay here, Leah. Work with me to change things." Yaakov wondered if the run-in with the soldiers had left her more disturbed than she had shown before.

"I have helped but it's gambling with my children's lives. Not any more. No, they need to grow up in a free country."

"This is all so sudden. Why?"

"My brothers wrote that we should come. Let's just leave it at that."

"I don't want you to go." There he had said it. Tentatively he took Leah's hand. The boy looked so forlorn, unable to comprehend what had changed her so suddenly.

"Dear Yaakov, I must." She removed her hand from his, her face resolute, unwavering.

She went into the bedroom and lay on the floor between the boys. Benny had made a ball out of twine which he was rolling to Joseph, who rolled it back, laughing and clapping his hands every time the ball came to him. When he saw his mother he crawled into her lap and put a hand on her full breast, his sign he wanted to nurse. She turned away from Benny and unbuttoned her top.

Today her children were safe and she intended that they stay that way. Imprinted on her brain was the image of the boy lying on his back, his eyes wide, his wispy moustaches making him look so young. She knew that image would be with her forever.

Going to America was the only thing to do. If there was a God, He had to know it too. Tomorrow she would send a letter to Simon and Dov begging them to please send funds for a boat passage for her and the boys. She would go to Holstein looking for the job he once promised, pleading with him also. Maybe he would even loan her some money. They would need to buy train tickets to get to Hamburg, where they would board an America-bound boat. To start their new life, she would sell the silver Kiddush cup and spice box, even the tortoise-shell combs. Soon they would be living in America with family and violence would become a dim, dark memory. The boys would go to school and have access to books and Benny would stop wetting himself every time he heard a loud noise outside. Joseph would grow up never having known the sound of gunfire or their neighbor, Mrs. Rozinski, screaming in the night.

They would also take with them memories of Morris, his love for his sons. She would remember the little girl buried in the cemetery outside of town. On the difficult days, when she couldn't forget the boy lying on his back, his eyes transfixed, she would think about her times by the Pripyet River, the afternoons with her father, games with her brothers, quiet talks with her mother before she became so ill. And she will treasure a slim book of poetry, along with the fragrance of oranges, to remind her of Vaselik.

If only she could close her eyes and whisper "Silva-Burka" and conjure the magic horse who could change her into a princess. But she knew that the power of magic horses belonged to another time of life. Now it was Leah who had to provide all the magic herself. She was ready.

1716222R00103

Made in the USA
San Bernardino, CA
20 January 2013